He looked at her carefully. He knew she would speak to him when she was ready. She always did. He carried on with his work.

"What are you doing?" she asked.

"Hoeing."

"No." She was cross. She wanted his attention.

"What's that stuff you're using?" He was sprinkling the earth with something from a bucket and then hoeing it in. He didn't answer. "It's nasty," she said. "I don't like it."

"I'm not surprised. It's not for little girls."

"I'm not little." But she had her hands behind her back and was swinging her long hair petulantly. "I'm a big girl."

He glanced quickly at her and went on sprinkling and hoeing. "Girls don't want to have anything to do with dried blood and bone meal."

"Blood?" She made a horrified face. "Ugh, Daddy. How could you?!"

"It makes the pretty flowers grow. . . ."

Other Thrillers
you will enjoy:

The Cat-Dogs and Other Tales of Horror
edited by A. Finnis

Hair-Raising: Ten Horror Stories
compiled by Penny Matthews

Thirteen
edited by T. Pines

BONE MEAL

SEVEN MORE TALES OF TERROR

Edited by A. Finnis

SCHOLASTIC INC.
New York Toronto London Auckland Sydney

No part of this publication may be reproduced in whole or in part, or stored in a retrieval system, or transmitted in any form, or by any means, electronic, mechanical, photocopying, recording, or otherwise, without written permission of the publisher. For information regarding permission, write to Scholastic Publications Limited, 7–9 Pratt Street, London NW1 OAE, UK.

ISBN 0-590-50982-9

12 11 10 9 8 7 6 5 4 3 2 1   5 6 7 8 9/9 0/0

Printed in U.S.A.   01

First Scholastic printing, December 1995

Acknowledgments

All of the stories are original and appear
for the first time in this volume.

The following are the copyright owners of the stories:

"Something to Read" copyright © 1994 by Philip Pullman
"Killing Time" copyright © 1994 by Jill Bennett
"J.R.E. Ponsford" copyright © 1994 by Graham Masterton
"The Buyers" copyright © 1994 by David Belbin
"Closeness" copyright © 1994 by Chris Westwood
"The Ring" copyright © 1994 by Margaret Bingley
"Bone Meal" copyright © 1994 by John Gordon

Contents

BONE MEAL

SEVEN MORE TALES OF TERROR

SOMETHING TO READ

Philip Pullman

ANNABEL WANDERED ALONG THE UNLIT COR-
ridor towards the school library, touching the
wallpaper lightly. There was one patch by the
secretary's door where it was torn, and she
had to skim over that bit without touching the
bare plaster, or else she'd have to go right
back to the corner and start again. One day
she'd had to do it no less than four times, and
she'd been late for Science as a result, and
had had to clean out the stick insects.

She paused in the lobby, where the noise
of the school disco was fainter, and read all
the notices for the fifteenth time before looking
out through the glass doors. It was nearly
dark. The remains of the day were staining
the sky red over the roofs of the houses on
the estate; little solid clouds coloured like
lemon, butter, and apricot floated even higher
up, against a background of navy blue. Annabel

stood there with one hand on the glass and looked out at them, like a teacher watching the playground.

Suddenly she became aware of a group of boys standing around a motorbike in the school gateway. She didn't recognize the one with the helmet, but the others were in her class, and she opened the door and called, "You boys! You ought to be inside!"

They looked away and said nothing, but the boy with the helmet said a rude word and the others laughed. She shook her head. Boys like that ought to be punished, but no one seemed to want to punish them.

She turned away and wandered across to the trophy cabinet. Nothing had been moved in there since 1973, no new names added to the tarnished silver cups and shields. It was a relic of the days when this had been a Grammar School. Annabel sometimes used to long to be back there, to be a pupil in those days, to see her name inscribed on the Edith Butler Shield for Dramatic Recitation, for example. But those times were gone.

She could see her reflection in the glass. She stood up a little straighter and tugged at the waist of her dress, pulling it down. It was too short; she had told them it was too short. It was dark green with a frilly white collar which was already, she thought, coming undone at the back. Why had they made her come? Her taste in music, as they well knew, was for the classics. No boy would want to dance with her, and she had no particular friends to talk to, even supposing you could talk with the music that loud. The whole experience would be *purgatorial,* she'd said passionately.

After a moment she wandered out of the lobby past the Assembly Hall and tried the door of the library. She knew it would be locked, but she felt a wave of bitter disappointment just the same. The one place in the school where she felt at home, and they locked it . . . And to make it worse, there was the latest novel by Iris Murdoch on the New Acquisitions shelf. Annabel had read all her others; she sometimes felt that Iris Murdoch had written *her.* She was longing to get her hands on this one, but the Sixth Form had first choice. As if any of them wanted to read it anyway! She could see it from here, tantalizingly close.

Annabel read so much it was like a disease.

When she didn't have a book in front of her, her eyes flickered restlessly all around, searching for print. She had always read: it was how she measured her life. When she was five, she had read Dr. Seuss; at seven she had gone on to Dick King-Smith and Helen Cresswell; by the age of ten she was reading Diana Wynne-Jones and Susan Cooper; and now at fourteen she was reading books for adults. Reading? Gulping down, rather, like those strange deep-sea fishes, all vast expanding mouth with a little ribbon of body trailing behind.

Anyone watching her would have thought that she actually wanted to consume the books physically. She took a fierce gloating private pleasure in opening a new book, in hearing the crackle of the binding, in smelling the paper, in riffling through the pages, in slowly sliding off the jacket; and while she read, her hands were never still: her thumbs would move back and forth, feeling the smoothness of the paper under them; her fingers would explore the mysteries of the hollow spine. Paperbacks were all right, but they broke easily. It was hardbacks that she coveted.

Yes, she was different from other people,

but what did that matter? Other people were shadows. It was books that were real. But her parents had formed the idea that she ought to get out more — make friends, talk to people — and they'd made her come to this disco in order to promote her social development. So here she was, drifting through the empty school while the hideous music thumped in the background. If only she had a book, she could sit quietly somewhere and read it. If she had a book she wouldn't get in anyone's way. She wouldn't bother anyone. Why did they bother her with their discos and their social development? Who needed social development when they had something to read? It would serve them right if she killed herself. And haunted them. If she was a ghost, she could read as much as she liked.

Someone ran shouting down the corridor, and Annabel sighed. Then she pursed her lips ruefully and shook her head. She caught sight of her reflection in the library door and tried the expression again, but it was too dim to see clearly.

What was the time? She peered closely at the gold watch on her thin wrist. It was a family heirloom; it had belonged to her great-aunt, who'd published a book of her reminiscences of life in East Africa, and Annabel was very proud of it. In the faint light from the end of the corridor she saw that it said half past eight. That meant — she counted it off on her fingers — eight forty-one, since she'd set it exactly at six and it lost a minute every quarter of an hour. Ages till the disco finished, then. Where else could she go? Everywhere was locked. Sighing, she touched the library door again and wandered towards the gym where the disco was being held, since there was nothing else to do. The noise of the music — if you could call it music — thudded brutally as she got closer. She took a deep breath, pushed open the gym door, and walked inside.

The noise was appalling, and so was the heat. They'd rigged up some coloured lights that flashed in time with the music, but apart from them the place was in darkness. It seemed like a suburb of hell, thought Annabel, inhabited by wild spirits who leapt up and down shrieking. It *must* be hell. She peered around resignedly. There was Mr. Carter the PE teacher, dancing energetically, or *bopping*, as she supposed they call it. And wasn't that Miss Andrews over there? She was wearing a rather revealing dress and a lot more make-up than she normally wore, but it was the English teacher nevertheless. Annabel made for her automatically.

"Hello, Annabel!" Miss Andrews shouted. "I didn't think you were coming."

Annabel made a face. Then she said, "This is like Book Two of *Paradise Lost.*"

"What? I can't hear you!"

"I said this is like Book Two of *Paradise Lost!*"

"Is it? Why aren't you dancing?"

Annabel gave a helpless shrug. She didn't think the teacher could have heard her properly. Then one of the older boys tapped Miss Andrews on the shoulder and jerked his head at the dance floor, and she nodded enthusiastically and went to join him. Annabel felt betrayed.

Someone shouted in her ear, and she winced.

"D'you want to dance?" came the shout again.

She turned to look at the speaker. It was a boy from her class called Tim. He was a decent enough boy, very ordinary, slightly plump; didn't read much. Why was he asking her to dance? Was he making fun of her? There couldn't be any other reason.

She curled her lip and said, "Whatever for?"

That took him aback. He stood there looking embarrassed.

"Well . . . I just thought I'd ask," he said. "That's all."

"Oh, that's all. I see. Did you think I'd enjoy dancing with you? Touching you, perhaps? Squirming and writhing and grunting? Do you think I want to look like *those* people? No, thank you. I'd rather die."

He had nothing to say. Finally he blinked and turned away. She might have felt triumphant, but something else had already come into her mind, making her flush with guilty pleasure.

She had remembered where she'd left a book!

True, it wasn't a novel; in fact it was a handbook about collecting and polishing semiprecious gemstones. But it was something to read. She'd got it out of the library on Tuesday afternoon, just before Games, and put it in her PE bag, which was still hanging on her peg. She left the gym at once, breathing fast, and made straight for the cloakrooms.

It was dark, but she found her peg easily

enough, and fumbled through the damp-smelling towel and clammy gym shoes till her fingers met the precious spine of the book. She hauled it out and pressed it to her breast. Now, where could she sit and read without being disturbed?

The moonlight outside the windows was bright enough to read by, surely. And it wasn't cold at all. She could go to the swimming pool: no one would want to go there.

Clutching the book to her side, she hurried through the corridors to the front entrance and slipped out as quietly as a shadow and around the side of the school. There was a hedge around the swimming pool, and a light high up on the school wall above it, just in case the moonlight wasn't enough. Everything was perfect. Even the hedge looked right: like a maze in a formal garden, a maze with a secret pool, hidden away, bathed in stately moonlight, where she could sit and read for ever . . .

She felt for the door, a two-metre-high piece of solid lapped cedar panelling, and nearly stamped with dismay when she found it locked. But she was too determined now to give up. Throwing her book over the door, to make it impossible to retreat, she leapt for the top, grabbed it, hauled herself up and jumped heavily down on the other side.

Panting with pleasure, she felt for the shoe that had come off, pushed back the hair that was hanging lopsidedly over her face, and stood up with the book safe in her hand. Her dress was rucked up, and she hauled it down absently. She was alone and the moon was shining. Everything was silver except for the shiny black water in the pool; even the dull square paving-stones looked soft, worn, antique — like real stone and not concrete.

And no one here but her! That was the best thing of all.

She turned slowly around, imagining a long silk gown fluttering loosely as she moved. She raised her left arm to see how the gold watch caught the moonlight, and thought how slender the arm seemed, how graceful even . . .

But she was already more interested in the book than in fantasies about her own appearance. Kicking off her shoes, she sat down at the edge of the pool and lowered her feet gingerly into the cold water, watching the moon's reflection shake itself like a jelly and little by little gather itself together in one piece. As soon as it was whole again she opened the book. If she held it fairly close it was possible to make out the words. Eyes wide, head bent low, she began to read.

A moment later, there was a rustling in the hedge. A girl's voice spoke quietly, and someone giggled.

Annabel sat absolutely still. She was furious: she knew what they were up to. Instead of replying, she bent closer to her book and hunched her shoulders. How dare they?

"Annabel!" said the same voice. It came from somewhere nearby.

Annabel took no notice. There was a whispered exchange, and another giggle.

"*Annabel!*" said the girl again.

Annabel put her hands over her ears.

"Ah, leave her, Linda," she heard clearly in another voice: a boy's.

"No! I don't want her getting in the way. She can go somewhere else."

Annabel recognized the voice, having heard the name. Linda was a girl in her class — pretty and popular and very nearly illiterate, as far as Annabel could tell. Annabel pressed her hands tighter, hunched her shoulders closer, glared at the book more intently than ever.

The hedge rustled again and the two figures stepped out, the boy more reluctantly than the girl. Linda stepped off the grass on to the paved surround of the pool and walked up to Annabel, stopping about a metre away. Annabel pretended to take no notice.

"Annabel, get lost," the girl said. "Go somewhere else. We was here first."

Annabel couldn't resist.

"We *were* here first," she corrected her. "I'm surprised to hear you still making that mistake. In any case, I'm busy reading. I hardly think I'm interrupting — "

"Oh, don't bother, Linda," the boy groaned, and now Annabel recognized him as well. He was called Ian, and she gathered that many of the girls thought him attractive. "She won't listen. Leave her alone."

"No, I won't," said Linda. "We come out here to mind our own business. She only come out here to get in the way. She can go and read her book anywhere, can't she? Why'd she want to come and get in the way?"

"I am not in the way," said Annabel.

"If I think you're in the way, you *are* in the way."

"I wonder whether you had considered the rightness of what you were doing before coming in here yourself," Annabel said. "If I were you I should go back to the disco and behave myself. I don't know what your parents — "

"I don't *believe* this!" said Linda. With a little fret of temper she stamped closer, right up against Annabel's shoulder. Annabel could smell her scent and the warm smell of her flesh, and wrinkled her nose before turning back to the book.

Ian hung back, unhappy. Linda nudged Annabel hard with her knee.

"Go on, get lost! All you want to do is read, so go and read somewhere else! No one asked you here! Just get lost!"

Annabel looked up at her coldly. Linda's eyes were bright, her breast was moving as she breathed quickly, the skin of her bare arms was gleaming smoothly in the moonlight.

"Certainly not," said Annabel. "I have every right to be here."

"*I have every right to be here!*" Linda jeered, imitating Annabel's precise voice.

"She ain't going to move, Linda," said Ian.

And Annabel hadn't moved an inch. The moon was still intact in the water, her hands still held the book on her lap.

But Linda had other ideas. She nudged Annabel again with her knee, harder this time, and the movement shook Annabel's feet in the water. The ripples slowly trailed out towards the moon.

"I can't stand you," said Linda. "You're a snob."

"I am not," said Annabel. "A snob is a person who apes the manners of those above them in society. It's not what you think it is at all. If you look it up in the dictionary — "

"Why can't you talk like everyone else? You stupid cow! Are you going to move or what?"

"I decline. And in fact, if you don't go back to the disco at once, I shall tell — "

Before she could say any more, Linda reached down and snatched the book from her hands.

"What are you *doing*?" Annabel cried, and began to struggle up, but Linda had flung the book out across the swimming pool. It fluttered like a wounded bird, and hit the water to float dumbly a few metres from the side.

"Oh! That's a *library* book!" said Annabel wildly. "It's not even *mine*!"

She knelt down at the edge and bent low, reaching out to try and paddle the water towards her. Linda turned away and stamped in disgust.

"Ian!" Annabel cried. "You've got to help! It's too far for me to reach . . . where do they keep the bamboo pole? Go and get it! Quick!"

He didn't move. Annabel leant out a little further. The book was bobbing lightly on the water and floating further away. She stood up and ran the few steps to Linda in a frenzy of anger and panic. Seizing Linda's shoulder, she shook it hard.

"Get that book! You just go and get it out of the water! How dare you treat a literary work like that, you barbarian! You illiterate savage!"

Linda, alarmed and angry, turned and shoved Annabel's hand away. Then Annabel hit her. The slap cracked loudly over the water. Breathless with astonishment, Linda gathered her wits and tried to strike back, but Annabel grabbed her hair and tried to force her into the pool. There was a moment of struggle, and someone shouted, and then Annabel herself lost her balance and, with a faint cry, fell in.

She sank at once. Swimming was not one of her strong points, but she knew that the human body tended to float; she could only suppose that the green dress was pulling her down.

She touched the bottom and kicked two or three times till she began to drift up again. At one point she felt the floating book with her fingertips, but she couldn't get hold of it, and then she was at the surface again. It wasn't at all cold.

She opened her eyes to see something amusing, as she thought: Ian and Linda kneeling side by side, peering down into the water with guilt on their faces. It occurred to her that more time had passed than she had thought.

And then she realized that she was dead. Well, wouldn't that serve them right!

There was no doubt about it. She got out of the pool and stood shivering beside them as her body floated up clumsily. Ian put his arms around Linda, and then changed his mind and reached out towards the body.

"It weren't my fault, Ian!" Linda said. "You

saw! She tried to push me in . . . Oh, this is horrible! What we gonna do?"

"She just fell in," Ian said stupidly. "You never pushed her . . . I better pull her out, what d'you reckon? Oh, God! Here, we better get Mr. Carter. You go and tell him and I'll . . . I dunno. Quick, go on."

"How'm I going to . . ." Linda gestured helplessly at the hedge.

"Oh, God! I dunno! Same way we come in! Go on!"

Linda ran to the hedge at the end and shoved herself at it blindly, while Ian paddled the water, trying to make Annabel's body drift towards him.

"I think the bamboo pole's over by the pump," said Annabel, but Ian took no notice. "If you grab the edge of my skirt you might be able to pull me a bit closer."

It was useless. He couldn't hear her at all.

"I don't think it'll float for long," said Annabel more loudly. "Probably my lungs are still full of water, which will increase the specific gravity of the body. You'd better be quick before it sinks. I'm not in any position to help at the moment. And it was entirely your fault, the pair of you."

It was no different, being dead. They still took no notice. She felt desolated, but that was nothing new either. You might have thought it would be quite interesting to be dead, at least at first, but it was worse than being alive. She didn't even want the book much any more.

Ian had given up trying to get her to float towards him, and was standing irresolutely by the hedge. He didn't look at the body. Annabel thought he looked frightened.

Then — it was like the feeling returning to a limb that had gone to sleep — she began to realize what it meant. She was dead. She was shut out for ever. Her future was snuffed out; the books she was going to write, her career as an author — it would never happen. She started to cry.

There was a sound of running feet and someone fumbling with the padlock, and then the gate crashed open. Mr. Carter came in with a rush and took one look at the pool and at Ian.

"Haven't you done *anything*?" he said.

He dived straight in, sending water splashing right through where Annabel was standing. He surfaced by the body, gasping, and lifted her head clear, then heaved her on to her back and towed her to the side.

"I'll lift her," he said to Ian. "You get hold and pull her out. Roll her over the edge. Come on, move!"

Ian hurried to do as he was told. Annabel hovered nearby, feeling irritated by their clumsiness. They seemed to be doing it on purpose to make her look ridiculous; they let her lank body droop awkwardly across the edge of the pool, streaming water from nose and mouth, as the sodden dark green dress bound her legs together. Ian hauled at one arm.

"For God's sake, boy, take hold properly!" Mr. Carter said, gasping with cold. "You'll dislocate her shoulder! Take her up gently . . ."

Annabel felt tears again. She looked down mistily at the poor dank thing sprawled wetly on the concrete, and saw Mr. Carter kneel beside her, take her head in his hands, and kiss her. She began to sob and moved away from the pool. There was a crowd gathering at the gate: open mouths, cruel wide eyes. She couldn't bear it.

She went back into the school and sat in the lobby. The disco music was still thudding from the gym, and it was clear that most of the kids had no idea that anything unusual had happened. Annabel didn't know what to do. What do you do when you're dead? Where do you go?

She felt bitterly frustrated. She wanted to explain whose fault it was, but no one would hear. She watched as things happened: Mr. Carter carried her body in and laid it in the Medical Room; Miss Andrews rang her parents; the police arrived, and then the ambulance; all the kids were sent home except for Ian and Linda, who were told to wait in the Head's study. Annabel didn't want to sit with them, so she went into the Medical Room to be with her body.

It had never been attractive, and now it was grotesque. One eye was open and the other half-shut; her mouth hung wide and wet; her legs and arms were stiff and awkward, like a puppet's. How dare they leave it like that? They must have done it on purpose. When she heard her mother and father arrive, she left the room. It would have been too embarrassing.

Instead she went along to the gym, where the lights were still switched on, and looked at the table where they'd been operating the disco. It was a complicated machine they'd hired for the night, with two turntables and a microphone and all kinds of switches. The records were strewn across another table nearby, and Annabel went over to read the labels. She was rather disappointed at how little information there was on them; she'd had the impression that record sleeves were covered in print. Perhaps that was just classical records.

Eventually the Head arrived and spoke to her parents. Annabel watched it all distantly. She still hadn't worked out what she ought to do. It was a puzzle.

When everyone had gone, and rather inconsiderately turned the lights out, she felt her way back to the lobby. She trailed her hand over the wallpaper, skimming the torn patch by the Secretary's door, but she couldn't feel it: she missed it twice and had to go back.

Then she noticed something very curious indeed. She could put her hand right through the wall. In the dim light from the glass front of the lobby, she seemed to be leaning on the wall with a stump. How peculiar!

After trying it gingerly once or twice, she stepped a little closer and tried to walk through. Without the slightest difficulty she found herself in the Secretary's office. It was darker in there, but she could still see quite clearly; perhaps it was never quite dark when you were dead.

She did it several times. It was really quite extraordinary, and yet it felt perfectly natural. Why, she could go anywhere . . .

She could get into the library! At last she could find something to read!

She turned and ran gleefully down the corridor. The whole library all to herself, and no one to tell her to go somewhere else or stop reading or do her homework or make conversation! It was almost worth being dead for that.

She stepped through the library door and paused a moment, with a little shaky sigh of satisfaction, gloating like a cat with a mouse. All those worlds that lay there on the shelves — all hers! Where could she start?

The new Iris Murdoch.

Licking her lips, Annabel moved towards the book greedily, reached for it, and missed.

That was clumsy. She tried again, and missed again. What was the matter with her?

She reached out tremblingly to touch the book, and her hand went right through it.

Then, all at once, the truth dawned. She would never be able to pick it up. She'd never be able to open it. In desperation she tried another book, with the same result.

She ran to another shelf, trying not to believe what was happening. She plunged her arms, her face, her whole body into shelf after shelf, trying to find something solid in the airy semblance of books that hung all around her; she even felt herself biting at them, trying to get at them that way, but her hands and teeth and arms met nothing at all — nothing but empty space. Finally, trembling, she stood still in horror.

All the books in the world were closed. Hundreds, thousands, millions of books, and all closed, and they would always remain closed. She would never feel that fierce joy of holding a book, smelling it, running her fingers through the pages, pressing her face to it. She would never be able to *read* . . .

Unless she stood behind someone and read over their shoulder.

But when she thought of the sort of books they *chose* . . . and how slowly and reluctantly they read, how eager they were to stop and throw the book down . . . face down . . .

Oh, it would be *purgatorial*!

Hadn't she said that before, about the disco?

But this was worse than any disco. Purgatory had been bad enough, but this was hell. And now she knew precisely what hell meant. It meant having all the books in the world, for ever, and nothing to read.

KILLING TIME

Jill Bennett

THE BOY TOILED UP THE HILL TOWARDS CROUCH Wood. The early afternoon sun beat on him unmercifully without a cloud to mask it, and sweat rolled down his back inside his shirt. He held the dead rabbit by its ears and from time to time felt its fur rub along his bare leg as he half walked, half ran to the fringe of trees ahead.

He had killed. He had done what he was ordered to do. But in spite of his elation his heart was thumping painfully and the tightness in his stomach told him that he was desperately afraid.

At last the trees surrounded him. Philip hardly noticed their cool shade as he ploughed on through the brambles and undergrowth until he reached a clearing where he stopped, breathless.

The caravan was still there — he had half

hoped it would be gone — and sitting on the wooden steps in front of it he saw, with a sinking heart, the figure of the White Man.

Philip walked slowly forward and held out the dead rabbit.

"Philip." The man on the steps stood up and took the limp body. His nearly colourless eyes stared at the boy, the white lashes planted in the pink rims, unblinking. Philip knew that he could see inside his very soul and stood before him, frozen.

"Good, Philip?" the White Man said. "Yes?" It was a question and Philip had to answer.

He'd twisted the rabbit's head and jerked its back legs the way his father had done many times out ferreting. The creature's back had snapped with a small crack and its body went limp. It had been good.

"Yes," he said and smiled.

"So." The White Man ran his hand through his thick white hair. "Now you know our ways, Philip. Now you are part of us, always." He reached behind him and picked something up from the caravan's steps. It was a shiny alarm clock.

Philip's eyes longed for it.

"This is for you. Once you wind it up, once

it starts to tell the time — your time — we will never leave you, ever. You will always have us for your friends." The White Man's mouth curved in a smile as he held out the clock.

Philip took it. Eagerly he turned it round to find the key in the back, but something made him feel uncertain. He looked up at the tall figure who was staring at him intently.

"Go on." There was a note of impatience in the White Man's voice. "Turn the key. Now!"

Philip did so and the clock began to tick. Gladness filled him. There was only one clock at home; he was going to be so important.

Satisfaction gleamed out of the White Man's odd eyes. "Wind the clock every day," he said. "Only you, mind, no one else. It will bring you back to us when you have to come. Go now, go home."

Philip turned and began to run. He burst into the sunny fields hugging the ticking clock to his chest.

Back in the clearing a figure came out of the caravan and went to join the White Man. Other figures stepped, like shadows, from the surrounding trees, until they were all standing in a circle, looking at one another silently.

                    *   *   *

It was so hot!

Nick kicked his duvet onto the floor and let the sweltering July night wash over him. He pushed his hair away from his damp forehead and shut his eyes, willing sleep to come.

Night sounds came in through his open window, but no air followed to freshen the small bedroom in the roof space of his house. Leaves rustled in the old cherry outside. It always rustled, even in the stillest night.

Nick turned on his side away from the sounds.

On this side of his bed he could hear another sound. A new one. It came from a battered old-fashioned alarm clock standing on his bedside table, ticking away. He opened one eye to look at it. Its face glimmered at him from a patch of moonlight. Once its chromium case had been shining and smooth, but now, with the years, it was blotched and roughened. It stood on three little legs and the bell for its alarm perched on the top like an oriental hat.

Nick had stolen it that afternoon.

He'd been ever so young when he'd seen the clock for the first time. Younger than Sally was now — much. It was the bell and the three little legs that had won his heart. He must have been about six, he reckoned as he shut his eye again and thought.

Granddad kept it in his garden shed, on the back shelf with the small spare pots and old seed trays. Nick remembered how he'd tried in vain to reach it.

"Here!" Granddad shouted at him.

Nick was so surprised to hear his granddad shout at him that he fell backwards off the box he'd climbed on and hit his head.

But that didn't stop him trying to get to the clock. To hold it in his hands, just to look at it.

Somehow Granddad always blocked him, but he didn't really mind. Being Granddad's A1 assistant, as he called him, was better than anything. There was always some project underway that called for his help. The old clock got forgotten for months at a time.

It was when Nick was eleven, like Sally now, that the next time came. That autumn they were having a big shed clear-out before winter caught them. Granddad had carried some rubbish down to the bottom of the garden where a bonfire was burning and Nick found himself in the shed staring at the clock.

He could reach the shelf now, if he stood on tip-toe, so he stretched up his arm and took it.

"Granddad!" he called to the figure half obscured by smoke. "Can I have this? Can you make it work?"

Nick wasn't prepared for what happened next. His granddad turned, saw what he was waving at him, dropped his fork and ran towards him, shouting.

"You put that back at once, boy! At once!" He reached Nick and snatched the clock away. He must have seen Nick's astonished face for he stopped abruptly and as suddenly dropped to his knees on the lawn beside him.

Granddad's eyes, on a level with his own, looked into his.

"Nick, lad," he said more gently, "I should have thrown that old thing away long ago. I don't know why I haven't. I don't expect it works any more anyway. But you see, it was my brother Phil's clock and . . . and . . . he thought the world of it, so I suppose I just let it be."

"I'll look after it, Granddad, honest. I'll polish it up and get it to go — you'll see."

"Nick," said his granddad again, "it's not

that I like the clock — I can't stand the thing. I never did like it even when Phil brought it home. He said it was sour grapes — a clock was a great thing to own in those days. But it wasn't. I just couldn't take to it, sitting in our room on the bedside table between the both of us — like it was watching us, somehow." He shuddered, remembering.

"Then why can't I have it?" Nick was puzzled. If Granddad didn't like the clock, then why?

Granddad sighed and got stiffly to his feet. He ran a shaky hand over his wispy hair and turned towards the shed. Nick followed.

"Phil was a bit older than you when . . . we lost him." Granddad leaned against the door post. "What are you now, eleven? Well, he was turning thirteen . . ." Granddad stopped and stared into the cobwebs in the far corner of the shed. Memories crowded round him. Nick cleared his throat.

Giving a little start, Granddad went on a bit more briskly. "When you're much older I'll tell you more. For now, that clock stays where it is, understand?" He put it at the back of the shelf with its face to the wall.

Nick nodded. He didn't understand at all.

"Tea time — Gran will be waiting," Granddad said firmly and headed back down the path to his cottage.

Nick watched him go. For the first time he felt a stab of anxiety.

He's old, Granddad is, he thought as he walked slowly down the path after him.

That was two years ago. Gran died the following winter and Granddad's life began to fall apart.

After that — Nick threw himself onto his back, anger muddled with confusion gripping him — after that, Granddad started to behave so oddly. Really stupid at times, he was. Everything used to be so great — they were such a good team. He'd even started to help him with difficult jobs like repairing the back fence. Now nothing ever got finished. Granddad would start something and then he'd wander off and pick up something else. Sometimes he didn't even remember that he, Nick, was there at all. Sometimes — and this made him feel really creepy — he'd even call him Phil.

That morning he'd gone over as usual and found Granddad staggering under a pile of old magazines and papers.

"Ah, Nick, lad," he said. "Just the man."

Nick felt hopeful. Granddad sounded like his old self.

"Take hold of these, lad, and stow them in the shed. I've a load of stuff to stow away today."

Nick took the bundle of old papers with a sinking heart. Granddad had taken to "stowing things" for the last few days. This really meant just moving piles of stuff from one place to the next. Since Gran died there was loads of stuff to move. Granddad never threw anything away.

This morning everything was going into the garden shed.

"Why don't we have a good bonfire?" Nick asked without much hope as Granddad heaved another load of papers and dusty books onto the little shed's floor.

"We'll fill the shelf first, Nick lad," he said as if Nick hadn't spoken. "You stack this lot."

So there Nick was, starting to cram the stuff on to the one shelf and staring at the back of the little clock once more.

It hadn't taken long to snatch it up and stuff it under his thick jumper.

"Silly old man!" he muttered as he quickly piled the shelves high. "It'd just get covered up forever. He'll never even miss it. Silly old fool!" Nick's heart was sore. He'd been such a friend, his granddad — they'd had such times.

So that was it. Dusted, oiled and wound, the clock was ticking beside his bed. The alarm bell spring had rusted through, but the hands were going round all right.

Nick wished he didn't feel so guilty.

Suddenly, like a light going off, he fell asleep. And with sleep came the dream.

Nick sat up in bed. The wind was lashing the branches of the cherry tree till they crashed against his window pane. It'll break the glass! he thought.

He peered through the window at the waving tree. The moonlight was bright outside, like day. Something was hanging from a branch, swinging in the wind. It was Granddad with a noose around his neck.

Granddad's face twisted up to look at Nick. It was bloated and horrible. As Nick watched, horrified, it melted into the face of a young boy who suddenly opened his eyes and stared at him. But his eyes had no pupils.

Nick woke up, sweating and shaking from the appalling nightmare, and reached for his bedside light. He looked at the clock for a clue to the time. It said ten past six. But there was no sign of dawn so it couldn't be right. Dimly he remembered that the clock had said ten past six when he first got it going. Perhaps it had been in that position for so long that it just went back there. He decided to set it right again in the morning.

"You look tired." Nick's mother glanced across the breakfast table at him. She was pouring milk over her cereal. "Sleep well?"

"Too hot," said Nick, his mouth full of bacon and egg.

"Hmmm," she agreed, thinking that her nights were not easy either. Her baby was due very soon, her husband was on early shift at the milk factory, and what with that and the heat . . .

"Crissy's done it! She's done it!" Sally, red-faced with heat and excitement, flung herself through the door. "She's got five — I counted!"

"I hope you didn't try to pick one up, Sal. Nick, come back here, the kittens will wait. Eat your breakfast . . ."

But he pushed back his chair and was making for the door.

"Three days, remember," their mother called after them. "You leave them be for three days." She sighed. Lucky Crissy, she thought wryly, although what would I do with five? Clever little cat.

It threatened to be hotter than ever. The thermometer in the porch already stood at 80 degrees and it wasn't ten o'clock. Sally's flop-eared rabbit, Freddie, lay stretched out on the grass in his run, panting slightly. Sally mooned over him, pushing long leaves of dandelion through the wire, but he wasn't hungry.

"Oh, leave him, he's just hot," Nick said irritably.

"He's my rabbit. I know what he wants." Sally began to sound truculent.

"Go and get me some eggs from the shop," their mother called at them through the kitchen window. Tempers ran short in the heat. "And get an ice at the same time. Ask Mr. Potts to put it in the book."

They sauntered off. None of their friends were around. Harvest time was in full swing and the farming families had a lot to do. Nick and Sally, in their small council house at the heart of the village, found the long summer days endless.

Licking their ice lollies, they paused to chat to old Mrs. Potts sitting in the shade of the shop wall, knitting. She loved a good chat.

"Dad still on earlies?" she asked them.

"Yeah," Nick said.

"You being good to your mum? Her baby's due any day."

Nick shifted impatiently. He didn't like being reminded about the new baby — it bored him.

"Mrs. Potts," he thought of something. "When you and Granddad were at school together . . ."

Mrs. Potts chuckled. "What times!" she said. "Your granddad now . . ."

Nick broke in. "What about his brother, Philip?"

"Ah," she said slowly, "that Philip. He was a rum 'un."

"Rum?" Sally sat on the patch of grass beside her chair, sensing a story.

"D'you mean he got into trouble?" Nick felt excited, he didn't know why.

Mrs. Potts laid her knitting on her lap and

thought how to answer, but Nick was impatient.

"He died when he was young, didn't he? Was it an accident?"

"I don't think as how it's for me to say how he died," Mrs. Potts said slowly. "None of us really knew at the time. It was ever so long ago."

"But you must have known something," Nick pressed her. "After all, you were all here together."

Mrs. Potts didn't like being harried. "You ask your granddad, not me, young Nick." She took up her knitting and flashed her needles busily. "Although I dare say you won't get much from him. It was a bad go altogether, and best forgotten."

"Oh, come on, Sal, let's go," Nick's frustration flared.

" 'Bye, Mrs. Potts," Sally scrambled up.

But Mrs. Potts wasn't listening. Her good-tempered face was creased with stern lines and she was saying something under her breath. As Sally looked back she saw her make the Sign of the Cross on her breast.

Sally suddenly thought of something.

"Nick," she called after her brother, "where did that clock in your room come from?"

"If I ever catch you near my room, I'll take that rabbit of yours and string him up by his stupid ears!" Nick turned on her viciously. "Leave me alone. Stop trailing about after me, little half-wit!"

Hurt, Sally stood watching him as he turned aside, climbed the stile into the sloping field, and made for Crouch Wood.

Nick was dreaming again.

He was standing beside Crissy's bed looking down at the kittens. He was holding one of the kittens in his hand. It was so tiny and it squirmed a little.

Nick felt its helplessness and wanted to go on squeezing it.

Instead, he put it down on the washroom floor.

He raised a foot to stamp.

He brought it down, hard — and woke up, screaming.

"Nick! Nick!" His mother's urgent voice made him sit up. "What's the matter? Was it a dream?" She sat awkwardly on his bed and put her arms around his shoulders.

Big though he was, Nick rested there gratefully. Revulsion tingled with the strange excitement he had felt earlier when he was
questioning Mrs. Potts made him shudder un-
controllably.

"Kittens . . ." he spoke thickly, "killing . . ."
He buried his face in her shoulder.

"There, there," she rocked him gently. "It's
this damned heat. How can anyone get a good
sleep in it?" And babies, and kittens, she
thought to herself. And harvest time too —
he's growing up and it's all too much. Poor
Nick.

"That's a funny old clock," she said to
lighten things. "It says ten past six — does it
work?"

Nick pulled away from her. "Sometimes,"
he said vaguely. A stab of fear went through
him. Would she tell Granddad?

"You could sleep outside on the patio if you
like. That would be cooler. You could take your
duvet and put it on the sunbed — come on."
She scooped up his pillow and made for the
door.

Nick followed, the horror receding. To get
out in the open, to breathe some air — that
was what he needed.

*   *   *

The boy Philip stood trembling with fear. He felt the rough fallen leaves of the wood under his bare feet. Terror and confusion flooded him. What was he doing here? Why was he wearing this white dress thing that came down to the ground? Where were his proper clothes? He struggled to remember, but when he tried all he could hear in his head was the ticking of the clock.

The clock! That was it. It had made him come, ticking off his hours, day after day, minute after . . .

"Philip!"

He tried to focus his eyes.

"Philip, willing and chosen," the voice continued, "we salute you!"

A shout came from the shadows standing round him.

Philip's vision suddenly cleared and he saw the White Man standing, tall, in front of a semicircle of shrouded black figures. He, too, was dressed completely in black, and his white hair flamed scarlet in the light of the setting sun.

He was holding a knife in both his hands, holding it out to Philip.

Philip stared at him. Then his eyes followed

the White Man's pointing finger and he gasped. A dog lay on the ground, still as death. Its eyes were not quite shut and its tongue lolled sideways from the half-open mouth. Philip could see its sides heaving with each laboured breath.

He recognized it. It was Jip, Farmer Brett's Jip, helpless and drugged, lying at his feet.

Understanding hit him like a thunderbolt.

"I can't do that!" Horror made him whisper.

"The earth needs the new blood, Philip. You know it does. Now, Philip!"

The White Man's weird eyes bored into his and Philip found himself reaching for the knife.

"You want to do it," the White Man said. "Want to, want to . . ."

The shadows around him took up the chant. "Want to, want to . . ."

Still Philip stood, like a white statue, listening to the noise of the chant all muddled in his head with the tick, tick of the clock.

The White Man's voice was low and menacing. "The dog, Philip — do it. If not the dog, it has to be someone else."

Splash!

Fat drops of rain, the first for three weeks,

dropped with small thuds onto Nick's duvet and defenceless face. As a low roll of thunder rumbled around the sleeping village, he woke up. He took a second to remember where he was, outside in the rain with the first streaks of dawn, then picked up his duvet and made for the house.

Without thinking too much about it he checked his watch and re-set the clock. Then he lay back on his bed and listened to its tick.

It seemed louder than ever.

Its insistent rhythm entered his mind and took him over. Soon it was all that he could hear or think about . . . all that he wanted to hear or think about. Half-heartedly he fought it, and for a second his granddad's face swam into his vision, but the ticking clock was too strong and he gave in to it.

Nick woke at his usual time, unrefreshed. The night's storm had made the air humid and heavy with moisture. But already the sun was back up there, burning.

Sally had finished breakfast when he came downstairs and his mother was washing something in the sink.

"Look, Nick, little boots!" Sally held up the tiny white garments and waved them at him.

"Mum's washing the stiffness out of the baby's nighties and I'll be in charge of keeping all his things tidy when he comes."

Nick felt detached. He saw his sister as if she was behind a sheet of glass, some shadow puppet he could hardly hear.

"Babies!" He spoke with limp contempt. "Useless things!"

His mother turned round, wiping her hands on her apron.

"Speaking as one who was one once," she said and smiled at him.

Nick's remote gaze regarded her coldly. He didn't bother to reply.

His mother watched him getting his breakfast things together, pouring his cup of tea, buttering his toast silently, deliberately, as if he was in another room, not part of them. She gave a sigh and turned back to her basin.

Sally put her head on one side and looked at her brother, a little puzzled. He didn't seem right somehow.

"What's the problem, Sal?" Nick said, his voice flat. "Your head too full of rubbish? It'll drop off at that angle."

He ate automatically, not noticing Sally's hurt at his snub.

When he had finished eating he took his plate and cup to the draining board and left the kitchen without a word. Crossing the narrow passage to the washroom, he walked towards the cat-box in its dark, protected corner. Crissy stretched her legs lazily as he approached her little nest. She knew him.

Nick bent over her as she lay in the blanket-lined box, her five kittens around her. They were sleepily nudging each other blindly, their new eyes closed tight. He reached out and picked up the nearest one. Crissy stirred and called to him but he took no notice.

He looked at the tiny ginger kitten lying in the palm of his hand and he closed his fingers round it.

The kitten squirmed.

Nick was back in his dream.

He began to feel his pleasure rise as he sensed the little creature's helplessness. All he had to do now was to put it on the washroom floor and . . .

"Nick! What on earth are you doing!"

Sally was standing at the washroom door, staring at him with horror. She had never seen Nick look like that before. "You've got a kitten. Its not three days yet!"

Coldly angry, Nick turned on her.

Sally quailed. She sensed the danger in him, but had to go on. "Give it to me — Crissy's crying." She held out her hand.

The mother cat, now very agitated, was mewing loudly and in Nick's palm the baby kitten opened its tiny pink mouth in inaudible reply.

Enormous frustration engulfed Nick. He could have smashed them all — he wanted to — but instead he put the kitten into Sally's outstretched palm, turned on his heel and made for the door. Here he paused and glared at his sister.

"If I catch you spying on me again these holidays, Stupid Sally, you'll be so sorry you'll wish you were dead!" He said this in a fierce whisper that was almost a hiss, then walked out through the garden gate and left it open. Ignoring the sun, he strode briskly in the direction of the hillside and the wood.

Sally put the little kitten back with the others and stroked Crissy until she settled. At the washroom door she stood and looked over at the hill where the distant figure of her brother was toiling upwards towards the gathering trees.

Nick had frightened her badly. He was so different — so horrid these days. But who could she tell about him? What could she say?

She would have to keep an eye on him in spite of his threat. She'd have to be clever and not let him know. Perhaps then she could find out what was going on, why he was spending more and more time alone in the wood, why he'd become so . . . nasty to her, to everybody.

Granddad came through the garden gate, shut it and waved to her.

"Your brother's in a hurry," he called.

Sally ran down the path to give him a hug. He had a basket of early plums on his arm and they both went gratefully into the cool kitchen to put the kettle on.

"That's better!" Granddad mopped at his face with a handkerchief. "Dratted heat!"

"I've never known it so hot!" said Sally, fetching mugs.

"I have. Can't stand it." Granddad was so emphatic. Sally paused, teapot raised.

The old man's eyes got misty. "It puts me in mind of a summer every bit as hot as this one. When we were boys."

"You and Philip, you mean?" Sally hoped this might be a story.

"That's right." Granddad sighed heavily. "Like yesterday, that harvest." Stirring his sugary tea, his face darkened as old memories swept over him.

"I've puzzled and puzzled about it — why it happened, why it started — and I can never work it out."

"What, Granddad?" Sally wanted to know, but she began to feel uneasy.

"We weren't alike, Phil and me. He was older and loved to be outdoors with the men working in the fields or ferreting and that. You wouldn't guess it now, but I liked to get away with a book. I was a bit of a dreamer, Mother said." He paused to take a sip of tea. When he went on again, he was obviously distressed.

"It was my fault. If I'd been different and gone out with him more — if I'd been more company for him like — he'd not have found those people."

"People?" But Granddad didn't hear Sally ask — he was back in that dreadful summer. She noticed his fixed faraway gaze and tried to bring him back.

"More tea, Granddad?"

"I don't know what it was about that . . . man. The Albino, we all called him — not to his face, mind, we wouldn't of dared. But Phil thought he was . . . wonderful."

Suddenly he looked straight at Sally. "He was never found, you know, that Albino. No one ever found him after he left — or any of the others."

"Found who?" The kitchen door had opened and Sally's mother stood there smiling, her hand on her large stomach.

Sally started, but relief followed. Granddad was getting very creepy.

The sudden interruption to his thoughts silenced the old man. Sally's mum came and sat at the table. She spoke quietly, with reassurance, so as not to alarm either of them.

"Pour us a cup of tea, Sal; I've a little wait till your dad gets here. I've phoned him and the hospital. Baby's on its way."

It was a boy. Granddad and Sally were over the moon and couldn't wait for their return home. Neighbours helped feed the children, who were left on their own during the long days. Sally read and played with Freddie but she kept her watching brief on Nick.

Nick had become more remote than ever, but at the same time he seemed agitated and was obviously worrying about something. Sally hardly saw him. He spent hours on his own, mainly up in the wood. When she asked him once what he did up there, Nick had muttered that he met a friend. Sally didn't believe him.

On one occasion she practised her stalking technique and followed him up the hill. She avoided treading on twigs and things that snapped, and slid from tree trunk to tree trunk. She was good at it.

He was there, sitting on an old log in a clearing, quite alone. He had his head up and his eyes shut as if he was listening to something.

It was very weird. Sally thought her brother looked enchanted, as if he was under a spell. She didn't dare let him see her.

Nick was listening to something. He was listening to the ticking of his clock. It was always with him now, either loud or soft or just inside him somewhere. It lulled him to sleep at night and ticked through the fearful dreams that always came to him. They didn't frighten him any more — he welcomed them. In the morning, when the clock had stopped and said ten past six again, he just wound it up and set it right. Voices came to him in the wood, mixed up with the ticking. They were luring, beautiful voices, enticing him with promises of wonderful things. But there was something he had to do first, something he wanted to do very much, the voices said. The clock would tell him when to do it. Just listen to the clock. The clock would know.

Every day his feeling of excitement grew. It was getting closer, he knew it. He began to cross off the days on the calendar. But, hand in hand with the excitement, came the dread. It always did. First the excitement and then the dread. It made him unable to join in with anything else going on.

He felt special — chosen — and he just wanted to be left alone . . . to wait.

Something told him it was very soon.

Something was telling him to go and find Crissy's kittens, that they were going to be needed . . . somehow needed . . . or one of them was . . .

Baby Peter and his mother had to stay in hospital longer than expected. There was some minor problem with the baby's feeding. Sally had been desolate but Nick was glad. He didn't want the fuss and clatter the new baby would cause and there was no way he could be made to touch it. Anyway, he was going to be busy.

Granddad came in daily. He seemed happy to be there, as if having to keep an eye on Nick and Sally while their mother was away was good for him. It kept him anchored and stopped him floating off into his past.

Three days later Nick found himself staring at Crissy's empty box in the washroom. He felt it — it was cold and had obviously been empty for a day or so. Rage filled him. How dare anybody remove the kittens just when he . . .

He flung himself into the sitting room where Sally and Granddad were watching a late afternoon film.

"Where's Crissy?" he demanded. "Her box is empty. The kittens are gone."

Sally looked at him, narrowly.

"Why d'you want them?" she asked.

"I want them. That's why." The tone of Nick's voice said, "You'd better tell me."

"Crissy didn't like you touching them. She's hidden them."

Sally had seen the mother cat cross a corner of the garden holding a kitten in her mouth and guessed that was why. She knew where they were, all right.

"Where?" Nick demanded.

"You're the last person I'd tell, even if I knew!" Sally retorted, meaning it.

Nick darted over to her, ignoring his grandfather, and grabbed her arm.

"Stop it! Ow, Nick, stop it!"

He had both his hands on her arm and was twisting her skin in a vicious Chinese burn.

"You're hurting me!" Sally's eyes smarted and her lip began to tremble.

Granddad, who'd been dozing during the film, woke up.

"Here!" he shouted at Nick in sudden surprise as he saw what he was doing.

Nick flung Sally's arm away from him. "Don't worry," he snarled at them. "I've got more than one string to my bow!" and he went out, giving the door an almighty bang.

Sally began to cry quietly. It wasn't just her smarting arm, it was Nick — the way he was now. Everything about him was horrible, and they had been such good friends — most of the time.

Granddad pulled out his large spotty handkerchief and gave it to her.

"What's got into young Nick these days?" he asked, rubbing her shoulder awkwardly.

Sally turned to him and buried her face in his shirt front, sobbing.

"There, there, little Sal," he said, quite at a loss. "I'll go and find him. I'll make him come back and say he's sorry. He shouldn't upset you like that. It's not right."

"Don't bother, Granddad, you won't find him." Sally rubbed her eyes. "He's off in the wood by now — he always is."

"In Crouch Wood?" Granddad asked. Sally nodded and blew her nose.

"Goes there a lot, does he?" Granddad went on.

Sally started to cry again. "He's always there, with a silly look on his face, sitting on the log in the clearing. I've seen him. He says he's meeting a friend in there, but he isn't."

Granddad took her gently by her shoulders and turned her to face him. "How long's this been going on?"

Sally tried to think. She remembered the day at the village shop and Mrs. Potts crossing herself. That was the first time he'd really shouted at her, before the business with the kitten . . . and that was all about . . .

"The clock . . ." she said out loud.

Granddad's grip on her shoulders tightened. "Clock? What clock?" There was nothing woolly about him now.

"He's got an old clock in his bedroom, really old . . ."

"Where'd he get it?" Granddad's look was frightening.

"I don't kn . . ." she quavered.

"Get it, Sal. Go on, now!" Granddad half lifted Sally up off the sofa and pushed her, almost roughly, towards the door. "Quick!"

Sally fled. She returned, clasping the clock. Granddad practically snatched it from her.

It said ten minutes to six.

"Has he got up there yet? Go look, Sal — see if you can see him."

Granddad was clutching the clock. He looked frozen to the sitting-room carpet.

At the open kitchen door, Sally's eyes raked the hillside. She just glimpsed the small figure of her brother before he disappeared into the trees of Crouch Wood. He seemed to be carrying something.

Then Sally screamed.

"Freddie's gone!" she wailed, looking at the open hutch and overturned run.

"Freddie?" Granddad was behind her. "Gone? Oh, Sal, I've got to stop him! This time I've got to stop him!"

Half running, half stumbling, Granddad set off down the path and into the lane, heading for the stile and the path to the wood.

Sally followed him, shouting, "Granddad, wait! We've got to find Freddie. Wait, Granddad!" But the old man didn't pause.

Golden light of the late summer's day lengthened the shadows imperceptibly, and the trees in Crouch Wood seemed to grow darker against it. Granddad's breath came in laboured gasps as he struggled up the steep incline. He knew it so well. As a boy he and Phil had done it many times, even raced each other up it, but now only his sheer determination kept him going. The clock was clutched in his hand and his only thought was to get to Nick in time.

Sally followed him helplessly with tears pouring down her face. Her shorter legs did not let her catch him up.

Nick stopped in the clearing, panting a little from the climb. He put the two plastic bags he was carrying down on the ground. One of

the bags had its handles knotted securely together and something inside it moved a little.

He stood in the centre of the clearing and
looked about him expectantly.

They had called him.

The clock had told him.

He had come.

Granddad stumbled into the ancient cluster of
trees. Crouch Wood let him through.

He leaned, gasping, against a tree trunk and
peered into the shadows. From where he was
standing he could just see the clearing and the
figure of Nick. Three steps further on and he
stopped again. Nick hadn't heard him. He was
listening to something else.

Granddad's eyes took a minute adjusting to
the shade after the bright sunshine. He rubbed
them, blinking hard, for his vision seemed to
blur. He thought he could see people slipping
from the surrounding trees. Black shadows
that slid across the open space to stand around
Nick.

He wanted to shout, to warn Nick, but he
couldn't move. It was like a dream where you
know danger is approaching but you are rooted
to the spot, unable to speak or move.

Nick looked as if he was in a trance, standing in the centre of the ring of shadows. Granddad watched helplessly as he bent down and picked up one of the bags he had brought. It held a length of washing line and a kitchen knife — one of his mother's meat knives, shining and sharp. The blade flashed for a moment in a shaft of sunshine and the ring of shadows wavered a little.

Nick laid it by and took the length of washing line, looping it into a noose. This he threw over a branch of a tree behind him where it hung down, swinging gently from side to side. It looked awful, that silent movement in the quiet wood.

Then he bent to pick up the knife again. It seemed to Granddad that he was obeying instructions, but who was issuing them? Was it the tall black figure standing in front of Nick, or was it the single figure in white who glimmered faintly beside him?

Nick was bending again and untying the second bag, working at the knot. Whatever was inside was making it difficult to do. It was lurching about with ragged movements, but as soon as he put his hand into the bag it became still.

Nick drew the rabbit out by its long ears and held it in one hand. It dangled passively, a hind leg twitching. The knife was in his other hand.

"Freddie!" Sally's scream shattered the wood.

Granddad could never tell what happened first. Was it Sally's scream or the white figure beside Nick who seemed to grab the knife and throw it hard away from him, and did both of them give that agonizing shout of *"No!"* Or was it Nick alone?

Granddad sprang forward, released by the shout. Nick dropped Freddie, turned to run, caught his foot on a bramble branch and fell. His head knocked against the tree behind him making the rope noose swing wildly, and he lay still.

They were alone in the wood. The fallen boy, the old man and the little girl who was sobbing and stroking her pet rabbit.

Granddad knelt beside Nick and turned him over gently. He straightened him up and bent to listen to his heart. He had nothing to cover him with or to put under his head, but he did all he could to make him comfortable. Sally came over and stood beside him, with Freddie in her arms.

"I hate him!" she said. "How could he do that to Freddie! I'm glad he's hurt."

Granddad sat back on his heels. His face was pale and drawn but he looked at her with clear eyes.

"It weren't Nick," he said. "Not our Nick."

"Who then?" demanded Sally.

"Old evil, little Sal; old, old evil."

Sally didn't understand.

"Years ago, the Albino gave this clock to my brother, Phil. I don't know what was in it, but it was nothing good. It changed him, just as it changed our Nick. You saw it. Whatever was put in that clock is still there, waiting for someone to start it up again."

He looked at the clock that was lying beside Nick's still form. It had stopped. Its hands said six o'clock.

Granddad went on speaking, almost to himself, as if he was finding the answer to something that had puzzled him for many years. "The day Phil died he was odder than ever, but something was worrying him too. I was reading a book in our bedroom when he set off to go to Crouch Wood.

" 'Bert,' he said to me, standing at the door, 'if I'm not home by six, you come and find me. Come, Bert, if I'm not out of the wood by then. Promise.' " Granddad's voice wobbled and trailed to a halt. He frowned to stop the tears that were forming in his eyes.

Sally waited.

"I forgot. It was ten past six when I looked up from my book, and the clock had stopped. I learned later that everything'd stopped for Philip too at about that time. I've never stopped wondering if I could have saved him, if only I'd . . ."

"Oh, Granddad." Sally's heart ached.

"I'm going to do what I should have done a long time ago," he said as he rose stiffly to his feet. Then he brought his strong old boot down on the clock's glass face, stamping till it was just a little pile of springs and glass and battered chromium plate.

"That's better!" he said. "That's done it!"

Then he turned to Sally. "Go off down, Sal, and see if your dad's home from visiting the hospital. We're going to need help with Nick. He'll be fine now. I'll stay with him till your dad arrives. Off you go."

Sally obeyed. She began to run, holding Freddie tightly in her arms.

Granddad knelt by Nick again and felt his pulse. It was slow and steady. He stroked the boy's forehead and picked a piece of bark from his hair.

His mind was still dwelling on the terrible day when they had found Phil, dressed in that white robe thing, hanging from a tree with Farmer Brett's Jip dead on the ground beneath him. It had been awful to think of what Phil had done to the helpless dog and then to himself. All these years they had thought it. He had been labelled mad.

He took one of Nick's hands and rubbed it gently. "But we know different now, don't we?" he said. "We saw what he did just now, our Phil, and those devils killed him for it."

Nick opened his eyes.

"Granddad?"

"You're all right now, lad, quite safe." Relief choked him.

"I'm in the wood." Nick's tone was disbelieving. "What am I doing in the wood?"

Granddad looked at his grandson's face. It was pale, certainly, but quite normal.

"You've had a fall and hit your head. Nothing's broken," he said with a reassuring smile. To himself he thought, you've forgotten all about it, our Nick. He sighed deeply. You've forgotten, but us, we'll all remember.

"Come," he said aloud. "Sit up slowly. Sally's gone for your dad, but perhaps we'll meet them halfway down."

Nick struggled up and stood with Granddad's arm supporting him.

"That's a boy," Granddad encouraged. "That's my A1 assistant. Come on, now — let's get home for a cup of tea."

Linked together, and leaning on one another, they made their slow way out of the wood and into the warm evening light on the hill.

J.R.E. PONSFORD

Graham Masterton

THE AFTERNOON SUN SLANTED THROUGH THE pale amber glass of the cricket pavilion window, and illuminated it like a chapel. Faintly, through the open skylights, Kieran could hear the knocking of bat against ball, followed by shouts of encouragement and ripples of applause.

It was Thursday, First XI *v* Milton College, attendance obligatory. But Kieran hardly ever went to cricket matches. In fact, he kept away from every school event where Benson and his friends could find him. He had been here five weeks now, since the start of the Summer Half, and Benson and his friends still chased him and ragged him as badly as they had on his very first day.

It had all started while he was unpacking his trunk. Marker, the head boy of Mallards'

House, tall and blond-headed and spotty and noble, had strode breezily into his room while he was unpacking his pyjamas. "Any good at eccer, O'Sullivan?" he had asked.

Kieran had studied the Heaton School information booklet for new boys carefully, and he knew that "eccer" was school slang for any kind of games; just as "ducker" meant swimming; while "short ducker", perversely, meant a cross-country run.

"I'm good at cricket, sir," he had volunteered.

"You're Irish, aren't you, O'Sullivan? All right then: name three famous Irish cricketers. And you don't have to call me 'sir'. You only call the beaks 'sir', and that's to their faces. Behind their backs you can call them anything you like."

Kieran had flushed. He was small for his age, curly headed, with a spattering of freckles across the bridge of his nose, and eyes as green as his mother's, green as those marbles they called "sea-green sailors". A scholarship boy.

"I don't think I know any Irish cricketers," he admitted.

"Well, exactly," Marker had told him. "But how about a house knock-about in the nets this afternoon?"

"All right," said Kieran. He had already been feeling homesick. His mother had seen him off at Shannon, and she had waved and waved until the airline bus had turned the corner around the terminal building, and she had probably kept on waving even when he couldn't see her. Ever since he had woken up in the morning, there had been a lump in Kieran's throat, and no matter how often he swallowed he hadn't been able to get rid of it.

On the plane he had closed his eyes and he had been able to smell his mother's perfume and feel her arms around him — his mother with her camel-coloured Marks & Spencer coat and her hair that was going grey on one side because of Stress.

"You've got some cricket kit, I suppose?" Marker had asked him.

"Yes, sir," Kieran had told him, and lifted out of the trunk the white V-necked cricket sweater with the yellow-and-brown house colours around the neck.

Marker had been looking casually out of the window, down at "yarder," three floors below,

where some of the boys were already playing
football. He had turned and smiled, his hair
shining godlike in the sun, and then he had
stared in disbelief.

"What on earth's *that*?"

That lump again; that unswallowable lump.
"It's my cricket sweater, sir."

Marker had let out a huge great shout of
laughter. "That's your cricket sweater? I've
never seen anything like it! My God, what
happened to it?"

His laughter had attracted two or three
older boys who were walking down the corridor. They had stopped and looked, and then
they had burst out laughing, too.

"That's not a cricket sweater! That's a cave-
man outfit!"

"You'll look like a Yeti in that!"

Kieran had clutched the sweater tight and
tears had prickled his eyes.

"We haven't got very much money, sir.
Granny O'Sullivan knitted it for me, from one
of the school photographs."

Marker had laughed so much that his face
had turned scarlet and tears had run down his
cheeks. The other boys had screamed and
yelled and kicked the panelled walls of the cor-

ridor. Kieran had sat on his bed and bitten his lip to stop himself from crying, his cricket sweater bundled in his lap.

Granny O'Sullivan had been so proud of it. She had kissed him and said, "Off to such a posh school, Kieran! Who'd have believed it? You'll be the smartest boy on the cricket-pitch, believe me!"

Marker had soon forgotten about the cricket jumper. After all, he was lofty and mature, an upper VIth, and above all that kind of thing. But the other boys — the Removes — hadn't. The worst of them all had been Benson, a swarthy, thick-necked boy with black curly hair and boils and a black silky moustache. Benson was the youngest son of the Benson Camping Supplies family. His brother had been head of school and captain of squash, and his father drove a bronze Bentley Continental R and gave absurdly generous donations to the Heaton School fund. Benson's mother wasn't his mother at all, but his father's third wife — a young blonde woman with deeply-tanned skin and vivid green short-skirted suits. Benson called her The Stick Insect.

Kieran couldn't imagine how Benson hadn't

been hurt by his father's divorces. Two divorces! Perhaps you got used to it. His own parents' divorce had cut him apart like broken glass. There had been so many rows, so much shouting, and then those long boring hours in the waiting rooms of solicitors' offices, with the rain pattering against the windows and the smell of old magazines. Then his father saying, with immense pride, those terrible words, worse than a death-sentence, "You're a lucky boy, Kieran. You've won a scholarship to Heaton."

So here he sat in the upper gallery of the cricket pavilion on this hot July afternoon, listening to the distant sounds of First XI *v* Milton College, dreaming and thinking and waiting for the hours to go by. A wasp flew in through the skylight and bizzled around for a while, and then flew out again.

Kieran took his mother's last letter out of his pocket. Pale blue Basildon Bond, with rubbery glue on the top of each sheet. Not like the heavily-embossed notepaper that everybody else received from their mothers, with house names like The Cedars and Crowhurst Lodge and Amherst. *My darling Kieran, I miss you so much. I go into your bedroom every day and turn down your bed, waiting for the day you come home. I'm sure you've made lots of friends, though. Rufus sends you a woof.*

He folded the letter up and tucked it back into his pocket. Gradually the sunlight in the cricket pavilion crept around, until it illuminated the tall glass case that stood in the very centre of the right-hand wall. Inside the case was propped a cricket-bat, a pair of worn-out pads, and a pair of old-fashioned wicket-keeper's gloves, as well as a faded black-and-white striped blazer, a First XI tie and a black tasselled cap.

Kieran stood up and walked across to the case and looked inside. He had looked inside it almost every day, because he always came here after lessons, so that Benson and the others wouldn't find him. He sat here and did his prep and ate apples and Drifter bars and sometimes he even fell asleep. It was the one place in the whole school where he felt safe and secure.

In the back of the glass case stood the oak-framed photograph of J. R. E. Ponsford, School Cricket Captain 1931–36. Public schools' champion batsman, 1935. A handsome, smiling boy, with dark brushed-back hair and amused-looking eyes. Kieran had liked him from the moment he had first seen him. At least he smiled. At least he didn't call him "Granny O'Sullivan" like the other boys. At least he didn't steal his tuck and spill ink over his prep and drop his towel in the mud.

At least he didn't make him cry.

The afternoon wore on. Kieran sat down in the corner and took out the fountain pen and the writing pad that his mother had bought for him at the corner stores. He had written home almost every day. *Dear Mummy, I am very homesick but I am sure that I will get used to it. I have been playing a lot of cricket and the maths teacher Mr. Barnett is nice. The food is not very nice we had grissle in the sheppers pie but I have plenty of tuck so not to worry.*

Lonely. He was so lonely.

But this time he looked at the sun-gilded case in the cricket pavilion, and then carefully wrote, in his best rounded handwriting: *Dear Mummy, I have made a good friend in the 6th Form his name is Ponsford. He has been very kind to me and takes me for net practice. He is the school's best batsman. He never rags me and won't allow any of the other boys to rag me either,*

even when they say things about me being Irish
or having a cricket sweater that granny knitted.

I am very happy here now so you mussnt
worry. Ponsford is coaching me every evening
so I expect that I will be chosen for the junior
cricket team. I must go now as Ponsford is
taking me for tea in the town.

He folded up the letter very small. It made
him feel better, writing a letter like that, because he knew that it would make his mother
feel better too. If he had actually known Ponsford, he was sure that Ponsford would have
been just like that, too: generous and kind and
protective. He imagined himself and Ponsford,
walking down the hill with their hands in their
pockets, chatting about cricket and what they
were going to have for tea. There was a place
called Café Café that all the Removes talked
about. Their parents sometimes came at
weekends and took them there for lunch and
bought them beer too.

He lay on the floor and rested his head on
his folded-up blazer and thought about playing
cricket. He was bowling, Ponsford was bat-
ting. The sun was going down over the oak
trees, and the late afternoon air was stitched
with midges.

"Well done, O'Sullivan, that was a cracking ball!"

He slept. His closed eyelids trembled. His thumb crept towards his mouth, but he didn't suck it. He hadn't sucked his thumb since he was three.

He woke up suddenly and the cricket pavilion was deep in gloom.

He stood up, and held up his wrist towards the window so that he could see what time it was. Oh, no! It was five minutes to ten. That meant that he had missed supper and callover and prep and everything! In a panic, he picked up his blazer and hurried along the gallery and down the stairs. He reached the front doors of the pavilion and tried to open them, but they were locked.

He rattled and rattled at the door handles but they wouldn't budge. He ran along to the far end of the pavilion, where they served the teas. All the windows were closed and locked; the door to the kitchen was locked, too.

He tried the ladies' toilets. Thank God, they were open! Even better, the window wasn't locked, either. He stood on the lavatory seat, climbed onto the windowsill, and opened it up.

He was balanced awkwardly for a moment, and his heel caught a tin of Harpic. It dropped with a clatter and a splash into the lavatory, and he waited breathlessly for a moment, listening, in case anybody had heard him. There was silence, and then the clock over Big School ponderously chimed ten.

O clock (as the school song put it) *that measures out each day*

Of diligence and carefree play!

He dropped down from the window onto the verandah. He twisted his ankle, but it wasn't too bad. He started to run and hop across the cricket-pitch towards the dark, Gothic outline of Mallards.

He took a short cut back to the house by running through the housemaster's garden. It was dark there, and heavily overgrown with sycamores, and with any luck nobody would see him. But as he ran round the back of the housemaster's garden shed, he collided at full tilt with four or five boys who were gathered in the shadows. Cigarettes were glowing in the darkness like fireflies.

"Hey, who's that?" yelped one of the boys.

A butane lighter flared. Kieran saw Muggeridge and Parker — and oh God — Benson too.

"God almighty, O'Sullivan. You smelly little bog-dweller. You practically gave me a heart-attack!"

"What are you doing out here? Shells are supposed to be tucked up in their beddy-weddies!"

"Yes, what are you doing out here, you little cretin? Spying, were you? Trying to get us into clag with Bonedome?" Bonedome was Mr. Henderson, their housemaster, who had an angular, bony head with five long strands of hair combed meticulously across it.

Benson pushed his way forward and shoved Kieran in the chest. Kieran stumbled back across an old rusty lawn-roller, and tore the seat of his trousers. He tried to get up but Benson pushed him again, and this time he fell right down between the roller and the side of the shed, scraping his ear against the splintery timber.

"You're a sneaky little cretin, O'Sullivan. What are you?"

"Leave me alone!" Kieran protested. He was already close to tears. He tried to get up yet again, but Benson this time punched him in the ribs.

"You're a sneaky little Irish cretin, that's what you are. You eat potatoes and you live in a bog and you say begorrah at the end of every sentence. And your old granny knitted your uniform."

Kieran managed to stand up. He said, "Leave me alone, Benson. I haven't done anything to you!"

"Oh yes, you have," said Benson, seizing the lapels of Kieran's blazer and screwing them around so that he almost choked him. "You've been breathing the same air as me, and living on the same planet. You're a horrible little apology for a person, O'Sullivan, and everything about you offends me. Everything!"

"Have you seen the bog-dweller's cricket bag?" put in Muggeridge. "Is it real rhinoceros hide from Louis Vuitton, do you think?"

"Oh, I don't think so," said Benson, fiercely ruffling up Kieran's hair.

"Is it canvas and pigskin from Slazenger, do you think?"

"I doubt it," said Benson. His face was pressed so close to Kieran's that Kieran could smell the cigarettes on his breath. "I know, O'Sullivan. Why don't you tell us where your cricket bag comes from? I'm sure we all want one just like it!"

Kieran was weeping now. He couldn't help himself. His ankle throbbed and his ribs hurt and his face was bleeding, and even more humiliating, his trousers were flapping open at the back and showing his underpants.

"Come on, O'Sullivan! Tell us where you got your cricket bag, and we'll let you go!"

"You know where I got it," he sobbed.

"Remind us," said Benson, ruffling his hair even more painfully. "I mean, it's got such a subtle label on it, hasn't it?"

"Dead subtle!" laughed Parker.

"It's just a plastic bag from the Co-Op," said Kieran.

"Did you hear that?" crowed Benson. "A plastic bag from the Co-Op! And we're supposed to live and breathe and rub shoulders and break our daily bread with a pathetic little Irish toerag who carries his cricket kit — his *home-knitted* cricket kit, in a plastic bag from the Co-Op!"

"My father's getting me a proper one," said

Kieran. "He's been away: he hasn't had time."

"Oh, your father's getting you a proper one? A plastic bag from Sainsbury's instead!"

"Your father's got all the time in the world!" Benson told him. "What your father hasn't got is any money!"

With that, Benson pushed him away. Kieran hurried off, smearing his tears with his hands. He had almost reached the back gate of the house when he heard footsteps rushing up behind him. The next thing he knew, Benson had kicked him in the back — so hard that he fell against the gate-post and almost knocked himself out.

"You're a bog-dweller, O'Sullivan!" Benson raged at him. "You're a smelly Irish peasant!"

Kieran hobbled into yarder, and miserably pressed the combination lock that let him into the house. As he pushed open the door, he saw Bonedome standing by the house notice-board, peering through his half-glasses at the cricket fixtures.

"My goodness, O'Sullivan!" Bonedome exclaimed. "Have you been run over?"

Matron dabbed his scrapes and his scratches with antiseptic, and gave him a paracetamol tablet and a glass of water. She was a bustling, friendly Australian woman whose husband worked for Qantas out at Heathrow Airport.

"Looks like you've been fighting, young man," she said, as she examined his cheek.

"Actually, I fell."

"Where from? The top of the clock tower?"

"I was late. I was trying to climb over the garden fence."

"You weren't down in the town, were you? Two Heaton boys were beaten up quite badly last term."

Kieran didn't answer. He had that lump in his throat again.

"You know what the Aborigines used to do, when they got the worst of a fight?"

Kieran shook his head.

"They used to make this special potion, and shake it over the spears and the loincloths of their dead warriors, and the dead warriors would come alive again and help them fight their battles. Spooky, don't you think?"

"Yes," Kieran managed to say.

Matron gently ruffled his hair. "You go and get into bed. I'll bring you something warm to drink, and then you can get some sleep. Leave your trousers out and I'll sew them for you."

Kieran said, "All right," but he had to turn his face away so that Matron wouldn't see him crying.

Dear Mummy, things are going very well. I am very happy. I have been playing cricket for the Juniors and Ponsford says that he has rarely seen such a good all-rounder as me (which of course made me pleased). I have still been getting some ragging from a horrible boy called Benson but Ponsford warned him to stay away and now everything is okay. Ponsford's parents are extremely rich and they have a large house in the country, Kent, I think. He has invited me to stay for the half-term with him.

My darling Kieran, I am so pleased that you are settling down so well at Heaton. We are all so proud that you are playing for the junior cricket team. Mr. Murphy at the corner store sends you his warmest congratulations! I am also very pleased that your friend Ponsford has invited you to spend half-term with him. It would be an enormous help to me if you could, since I am rather short of £££ at the moment — usual   problem!!! — and   it would certainly save the air-fare.

It was half-term. Kieran stood in the upper gallery of the cricket pavilion with his face pressed against the glass display case, staring at the photograph of J. R. E. Ponsford. He tried to imagine what they might be doing together. Going to McDonald's for a Big Mac and a large milkshake? Practising cricket in Ponsford's huge, tree-shaded garden? Perhaps they would go swimming in the lake, and then have a big tea, with cakes and everything.

On the floor was a heap of cushions and blankets, and a bag filled with chocolate bars and crisps. He had been living off sweets and crisps for two days now, and he felt hungry and sick. He would have done anything for a hamburger or some fish and chips, but he didn't dare leave the pavilion in case one of the beaks caught sight of him. He knew that Mummy didn't have much money but he wished and wished that he hadn't made up that bit about Ponsford inviting him home for the holidays.

Next to his blankets was a small stack of

books: *The Australian Outback, The Look-and-Learn Book of Aborigines, Nyungar Tradition* and *Thorn Bird Country*. He had taken them out of the school library before half-term, and he had already found two mentions of the story that Matron had told him, about the potion that could bring dead warriors to life. It was part of the frightening *kadaitcha* magic practised in Queensland. The blood and the feathers of a bird were mixed with mud and crushed-up bone, while the sorcerer chanted *epuldugger, epuldugger,* which meant "come to the place where the dead spirit rises up and takes revenge."

In Australia, the potion was made with emu feathers and emu blood, and the bones were either human or kangaroo. But Kieran didn't think that it would make any difference if he used any old bird, or any old bone. It was the magic that counted, the *kadaitcha,* the determination to do harm.

He unwrapped another Crunchie and ate it without enthusiasm. J. R. E. Ponsford smiled at him kindly from his glass case as if he were saying, "Chin up, old man! You can do it!" But Kieran stared back at him dejectedly and wondered whether he could.

*   *   *

On Sunday evening, the school grounds were noisy with Range Rovers and Jaguars and BMWs as the rest of the boys returned from their half-term holiday. Kieran hid in the house changing rooms until a quarter to nine, and then skirted around the outside of Mallards, and walked in through the front door as if he had just arrived.

"Good holiday, O'Sullivan?" Bonedome asked him. "And how was Ireland?"

"Full of bog-peasants, as usual!" Benson remarked, pushing past them.

Bonedome gave an indulgent laugh. He didn't wait for Kieran to answer his question, but turned to a senior boy and said, "Congratulations on your father's CBE, Mason! You must be very proud of him!"

The bell rang for supper. Kieran was so hungry that he could hardly wait. He left the house and jogged across the fields and up the wide stone steps to the main school dining hall. A few other boys were running from other houses, too — from Carlisle's and Headmaster's — so that they could be first in the queue.

The clock on top of Big School chimed nine,

and a flock of starlings turned and wheeled around the clocktower. The school rooftops had been plagued with starlings this year; and it was a starling that Kieran had found this morning, limping along the verandah of the cricket pavilion with a broken wing. He didn't like to think about what he'd done. He could still see its eye staring accusingly at him.

He managed to be fifth in the queue in the dining hall. It was sausages tonight, as it always was on the nights they returned to school from half-term holidays. Kieran asked for three, with heaps of baked beans and mashed potatoes. He carried his plate carefully back along the line of jostling boys. The dining hall was filling up now, and the noise of laughing and hooting and shouting was almost deafening.

Kieran had almost reached the house table when somebody tripped him. He staggered, nearly caught his balance, but then his whole plateful of supper dropped onto his shirt and down his trousers. The plate dropped too, and broke in half.

"God!" said Benson. "These bog-peasants are so stupid they can't even carry a plate!"

Kieran took a whole handful of beans and

mashed potato from the front of his shirt and threw it in Benson's face. There was a huge roar of laughter, and a shout of "Fight! fight! fight!" Benson lunged at Kieran but Kieran dodged away, and then ran for the door.

"I'm going to kill you for this!" screamed Benson. He turned to Muggeridge and Parker, and said, "Come on, let's sort him out once and for all!"

Kieran flew down the steps outside the dining hall three at a time. But instead of running back towards the house, he vaulted the rosebeds that lined the pathway, and cut diagonally across the cricket pitch towards the pavilion. He ran as fast as he could, his shoes drumming on the hard grass. *Epuldugger, epuldugger!* Help me! *Epuldugger, epuldugger!* Help me!

He heard Benson and his friends running along the path. The far side of the pitch was so shadowy that they obviously couldn't see him at first. He had almost reached the safety of the pavilion when he heard Muggeridge whooping, "There he is! Bog-peasant halloooo!"

Kieran ran around the pavilion to the toilet window. He dragged one of the heavy wrought-iron benches across, and climbed up

on it, and scrambled onto the windowsill. He
caught his pocket on the handle, but he managed to disentangle himself and drop down into
the Ladies. He crossed the main pavilion floor
and ran up the stairs.

Benson and his friends reached the pavilion
only a few moments later, panting and swear-
ing. Parker noisily shook the front door-han-
dles, but the door was locked. Then they ran
round to the back and tried the back door, but
that was locked, too.

"Where's he got to, the little cretin?" Benson demanded. "I'm going to wring his neck
when I catch hold of him!"

It was then that Muggeridge caught sight of
the open window. "There! He's climbed in
there!"

"Then he's caught like a rat in a trap, isn't
he?" said Benson.

The three of them climbed in through the
window. They were much bigger and heavier
than Kieran, and they were gasping by the
time they had managed it.

"It isn't half dark. Where is this?"

"It's the Ladies' loo, for God's sake! Hey,
careful! I nearly put my foot down it."

They crossed the pavilion floor. It was only ten past nine, but the evening was cloudy, and the interior of the pavilion was thick with clotted shadows.

"Any lights anywhere?" asked Muggeridge; but Benson said, "Better not. This is out of bounds except during cricket matches. Don't want the groundsmen coming around to find out who's in here."

Treading as quietly as they could, they reached the stairs.

"I'll bet you anything he's hiding up there."

They listened. The pavilion was silent, except for their own breathing and the occasional creak of an old timber.

Upstairs, at the very end of the gallery, Kieran was standing next to the glass display case. His chest was rising and falling because he had been running so hard, but he was completely calm, completely determined. He whispered, "*Epuldugger, epuldugger,* come to the place where the dead spirit rises up and takes revenge."

He unscrewed the jamjar which he had hidden behind the display case, and dipped his fingers into the potion. It was sticky and it smelled strongly of blood and rugby-field mud.

"Epuldugger," he chanted, louder this time. *"Crumbana coomera.* I give blood to the dead man. The dead spirit rises up and takes revenge."

With two fingers, he painted his potion all around the mahogany frame of the cabinet. *"Epuldugger,* help me!" he breathed. He closed his eyes as tight as he could, trying to believe, trying to believe. Tears ran freely down his cheeks. *"Epuldugger,* help me!"

He opened his eyes again, and unfastened the brass catch on the display-case door, and swung it open. The glass momentarily reflected the pale, moonlike clock-face on the top of Big School. Inside the case it smelled of old, musty clothes and varnish.

Ponsford's cap, Ponsford's blazer, Ponsford's cricket-flannels, all neatly folded. Ponsford's record-breaking cricket-bat.

"Epuldugger," wept Kieran. *"Please!"*

Downstairs, Benson and his friends approached the foot of the staircase. "O'Sullivan!" Benson shouted. "We know you're up there, O'Sullivan! You'd better give yourself up before we come up and do something you seriously wouldn't like!"

They listened again, but all they could hear was the faintest scratching sound, and that could have been anything — a mouse or a bird.

"Come on," said Benson. Taking one slow step at a time, he began to climb the stairs, and his friends followed. They reached the upper gallery and stood peering into the amber-tinted gloom.

"O'Sullivan? Come on, O'Sullivan. We're missing our supper because of you, and that could mean death, or even worse."

"I say we lock the toilet window so that he has to stay here all night," Muggeridge suggested.

"I say we find the little bog-dweller and beat him up," Benson insisted.

They took two or three steps forward. They stopped, straining their eyes, straining their ears.

"They've got a natural talent for cowardice, these Irish peasants," said Parker. "It's all they're any good at."

Benson said, *"Ssh!"*

They heard a slight scuffling sound. Then two sharp knocks. Then they heard somebody walking towards them; and what was strange was the rattling, rumbling noise that his shoes made on the parquet flooring. The sort of noise that cricket-studs made.

Out of the shadows at the very far end of the gallery, a tall figure appeared. He was dressed all in white, and his face was white, too — as white as a photograph, as white as death. Most unnerving of all, his eyes were closed, and yet he walked towards them without any hesitation whatsoever.

He was wearing a black cricket cap, emblazoned with the HS insignia of Heaton School, and he was carrying a cricket bat. He wasn't carrying it casually, either. It was already raised to waist-level in both hands, as if he were just about to hit a fast, hard ball from the other end of the pitch.

"Who the hell are *you*?" said Parker, but his voice was very much shriller than usual.

The young man in white didn't break his rattling, studded stride for even a second, even though his eyes remained closed. He came towards Parker at a fast walking pace and hit him on the side of the head with his cricket bat, with a terrible knocking sound that echoed all around the gallery.

Parker dropped to the floor without a sound. Muggeridge started to kneel down beside him, then thought better of it, but it was too late. The young man hit him across the shoulders, and then again, on the back of the head, and then again, and again, and Parker's right ear was reduced to a smashed piece of red gristle.

Benson, whining, tried to dodge back towards the stairs. But the young man in white came relentlessly after him, raising his bat high.

"Go away! Leave me alone!" Benson shouted at him, hoarsely. "You're mad, go away!"

The bat swung and hit him hard on the left shoulder.

"Leave me alone! Leave me alone!" he screamed.

The batsman hit Benson again, and this time his collarbone audibly snapped. He whimpered, and ducked, and turned, and tried to run towards the stairs, but Kieran was standing there, almost as pale as the cricketer, his eyes wide and staring, his hands raised, palms outwards, as if he were praying, or invoking a spirit.

"For God's sake, O'Sullivan!" Benson screamed at him.

But then the batsman hit him on the side of the head with a blow that would have sent a cricket-ball way past the boundary, over the roof-ridge of Big School, and out of sight. The end of the bat split. Benson's skull cracked, and he spun around and collapsed onto the floor.

Kieran stood over him, saying nothing, his hands still raised. He looked up at the silent white figure who was motionless now, white as a photograph, white as death. Tears sparkled in Kieran's eyes.

"Thank you," he whispered. "Thank you, thank you, thank you."

Kieran's mother sat in the housemaster's office holding her white vinyl handbag and looking pale. One of the senior boys, not realizing who she was, had remarked to his friends how pretty she was: a "yummy Mummy" as they always called them. He hadn't had time to evaluate the Marks & Spencer summer dress or the cultured pearl necklace.

Bonedome sat behind his desk and steepled his hands and tried to look sad but sympathetic. This was almost impossible for a man who had never truly felt either emotion in the whole of his life, and resulted in an extraordinary grimace, as if he had just bitten into a lemon.

"You understand that Kieran will have to be suspended during the police investigation," he said. "We can't possibly risk any kind of repetition."

"But why Kieran?" asked his mother. "He told me on the phone that Ponsford did it."

Bonedome took off his glasses. "I'm sorry? Ponsford?"

"He said his friend Ponsford did it, to protect him. He said that Benson and the others had been bullying him, and so Ponsford had taught them a lesson. I mean — I know what he did was terrible, it went far beyond anything he should have done — but why suspend Kieran?"

"Ponsford," said Bonedome. Then, *"Ponsford?* We have nobody at Heaton named Ponsford."

"Well, that's ridiculous," said Kieran's mother, shaking her head and smiling. "Pons-

ford has been Kieran's closest friend ever
since he's been here . . . he's been teaching
him cricket . . . Kieran spent the half-term
holiday with him. J. R. E. Ponsford, Upper
Sixth, captain of cricket."

Bonedome blinked. "J. R. E. Ponsford? J.
R. E. Ponsford, captain of cricket?"

"Then you *do* know him?"

"My dear Mrs. O'Sullivan, everybody at
Heaton knows J. R. E. Ponsford. He was the
greatest cricket champion the school ever pro-
duced."

Kieran's mother's smile faded away. "*Was?*"
she said.

"I'm afraid so, Mrs. O'Sullivan. J. R. E.
Ponsford was educated at Heaton from 1931
to 1936. Subsequently, he joined the RAF as
a bomber pilot, and went missing over the
Dutch coast in the winter of 1942."

Kieran was still standing in front of the glass
display case in the cricket pavilion when his
mother came to take him home. She put her
arm around his shoulder, and held him close,
and she still smelled like Mummy.

"I'm sorry," she said.

Kieran said nothing, but looked for the last time into the bright open eyes of J. R. E. Ponsford, and down at his famous cricket bat. A five-centimetre crack bore witness to his last and greatest match.

THE BUYERS

David Belbin

DOWN THE STREET, A DOG BEGAN TO BARK. Karen couldn't concentrate. Her homework was due in tomorrow and Mr. Briggs would knock off marks if it was late.

The noise the dog made was an insecure, high-pitched yelp. It would bark for a minute or more, rest for ten seconds or so, then start up again, making thought impossible. It was probably lonely, scared, or both, and she ought to be angry with the owners, not the dog. But she had exams in a few months. She couldn't afford to be sympathetic.

The dog barked again. Karen threw her pen across her desk, stood up and marched over to the sash window. Pulling the top half down, she leant out into the dank, overcast afternoon and yelled.

"Shut up! For heaven's sake, stop it!"

In reply, the dog barked again. Now a second dog began to bark, from the other side of the street. A moment later, a third joined in. This one was much louder and fiercer. Karen felt like crying.

She knew what was coming next: a deep, ominous howl. This was the noise made by the guard dogs up the road, roaming the small private park which surrounded Bob Bosco's home. Bosco was a well-known comedian, but Karen didn't find him very funny. She didn't know why he had chosen to live in this grotty area, where he had been brought up, or why he needed to surround his house with vicious dogs.

Slamming the window shut, she threw her school things into a carrier bag and marched downstairs.

"I can't work in this house any more!" she announced to Mum, who was watching the TV news. "I'm going to go to the library."

"Karen, hold on."

Karen already had the front door open.

"I can't stand living round here any more," she moaned, holding back tears of frustration. She looked outside, where the paint on the "For Sale" sign was beginning to peel. "Why won't anyone come and buy our house, Mum?"

"Eventually they will, love. Some things take time."

"And some things take *forever*," Karen complained. "We've had the house on the market six months. No-one in their right mind would want to live here. Look at it!"

She pointed at the dog muck on the bumpy pavement. A crisp packet tumbled along the street in the wet, dirty breeze.

"Face it, Mum. This place has gone to the dogs!"

"It's not as bad as all that," Mum told her. "The market will pick up. The recession's meant to be ending."

"Dream on," Karen said. "Anyway, I'm going to the library."

"That's what I was trying to tell you. You can't."

"Why not?"

"Because the library doesn't open in the evenings any more. Not since February. Cuts."

"I don't believe it!" Karen kicked the door in frustration.

"I'm sorry, love." She paused. "Listen — the dogs have stopped barking. Why don't I make us a coffee, then you can get on with your work?"

Karen shrugged. "Doesn't look like I've got much choice, does it?"

"Shut the door, then. The cold's getting in."

As Karen turned to close the door, she heard the creak of the front gate opening. Two grey shadows blocked out the light in the hall.

"Excuse us."

The two people standing in the doorway didn't look like door-to-door canvassers. Nor did they look like Jehovah's Witnesses. Each wore a dull grey mac. Karen wondered if they were friends of her parents, but it soon became apparent that Mum didn't know them.

"Can we help you?" Mum asked.

"We'd like to look around your house," the man said in a polite voice. "If that's all right."

"Er, yes," Mum answered enthusiastically. "Of course." Karen felt uneasy.

"What about Dad?" she pointed out. "He's in the bath."

"Oh. Right."

Mum got very nervous when potential buyers came round. Not that there had been many of them.

"Would it be possible," Mum asked awkwardly, "for you to come back in a short while — say, half an hour? My husband's in the bath and — you know how it is — we need to straighten things up."

The man, who was in his thirties, looked at his watch.

"In half an hour," he said, in an accent which Karen couldn't place, but wasn't local. His wife or girlfriend (Karen couldn't see if she wore a ring) nodded. The couple turned slowly away, closing the gate behind them as they left.

"I thought we were only meant to take people who come through the estate agent," Karen queried, once they'd gone. "It says *By Appointment Only* on the sign."

"Beggars can't be choosers," Mum replied, then yelled up the stairs. "John! Get out of that bath. We've got people coming round to look at the house in a few minutes." She turned to Karen.

"Forget your essay for now. Get the vacuum cleaner out. And never say such horrible things about the area while the front door's open. You'd better pray that they didn't overhear you."

Karen did as she was told. These were the

first potential buyers to visit in nearly two months. The Connors had all become careless about keeping the place spick and span. Selling the house took priority over everything else. Twice, they'd reduced the price.

"Any lower," Dad complained, "and we'll be giving it away!"

The house they wanted to buy was a big old semi, with large rooms, a garage and a garden. It was on a quiet, tree-lined street on the posher side of town, nearer school and nearer to Karen's boyfriend, Mike. Now that Mum had started working full-time again, they could afford somewhere better. The cost of this new house would stretch her parents to the limit, but Karen didn't care if she would have to sacrifice holidays or new clothes. All she wanted was to get out of this dump and live somewhere nice for a change.

"Get that muck off the floor now. I want to vacuum!" Max, Karen's younger brother, jumped as she swept into the room.

"Come on, move!"

Max began to clear his comics away frantically. He didn't need to ask what it was about. There was only one thing which would make Karen go anywhere near a vacuum cleaner.

He was fed up with his cramped attic room. There was barely room for him and his computer, never mind his friends. He wanted to move almost as badly as she did. When Karen suggested that he go into the bathroom and clean out the toilet, he obeyed without a murmur of complaint.

Twenty minutes later, the house resembled a show home. Karen was putting the feather duster away when the doorbell rang.

"You answer it," Mum called from the kitchen. She was putting some frozen part-baked rolls into the oven. The idea was for pleasant smells to fill the house, tempting the visitors.

Karen opened the door and smiled tentatively. The woman gave an awkward grin. She was younger than the man. No more than thirty, Karen thought, and pasty-faced, as though she spent most of her time indoors. Her hair was dark and dull.

"Come in, Mr. and Mrs. . . . ."

They didn't supply their name. Oh heck, thought Karen, as the couple walked into the hallway. Suppose they're sister and brother? The plain-looking woman, she saw now, was not wearing a wedding ring.

"Can I take your coats?" she asked.

"No," the man replied. "We're fine, honestly."

Karen heard Mum closing the oven door. Where was Dad? He usually showed people around.

"This is . . . er, the hall," she explained. "Perhaps you'd like to see the kitchen first. My mother's in there." But the potential buyers had already walked into the living room.

Dad bounded down the stairs. There was dust sticking to his hair. He had been clearing the entrance to the loft, in case these people wanted to look at it.

"Hi!" he said, in his slightly fake, booming, friendly voice. "I'm Bob Connor. Can I show you around?"

"Your daughter is already doing a good job, thank you," said the man. He had the trace of an accent, but Karen couldn't place it.

"Oh, well then . . ."

Karen and her dad exchanged looks. She never showed people around. However, you didn't do anything to irritate a potential buyer.

"You know where everything is?" Dad asked, in a low voice.

"Sure." She had listened to him giving peo-

ple his spiel about the house often enough to
know it by heart.

"There's a telephone point over there. And
two double power points. The fireplace is an
original feature."

She blathered on, though the couple showed
no obvious interest in what she was saying.
Karen followed them as they left the room and
started to walk upstairs. She'd intended to
show them all over the ground floor first, so
that Mum could take over when they got to
the kitchen. Instead, they walked straight into
her bedroom and stood by the window, looking
out over the estate to the small park beyond.
Outside, thankfully, the dogs were still quiet.

"That park you can see from here — the
comedian Bob Bosco lives there. He was born
in this area, you know, before the estate was
built. He says he likes to keep close to his
roots."

The couple showed no interest in this piece
of information. They examined Karen's book-
shelves, her single bed and the old radiator
beside it. The woman tested the lock on the
door from both sides, then peered closely at
the bedside photo of Karen's boyfriend, Mike,
with his freckled face and curly ginger hair.

The new house was only five minutes' walk from Mike's. Karen would be able to see more of him. If . . .

She ought to be used to it by now, but somehow she never got over how embarrassing it was, the way people could just come in and inspect all your possessions. It was like finding a stranger reading your diary. Nevertheless, she continued to talk, acting the estate agent.

"The original sash windows work perfectly and the house was rewired only three years ago. So it's all in excellent condition."

The man lifted up a corner of carpet where the tack holding it down had come up. He gripped the floorboard beneath and yanked the sides, as though trying to see if it would come loose.

There were questions that you were supposed to ask prospective purchasers: were they first-time buyers? If not, had they sold their own house? Was there a chain? But Karen felt too intimidated to ask these people and she doubted whether they would answer if she did. In order to keep calm, she kept thinking about the room that would be hers in the new house. It overlooked the garden instead of a yard, and had its own TV point.

The couple glanced at Mum and Dad's room. Then Karen offered to show them Max's attic room and the loft space, but they ignored her and shuffled back downstairs. They're not interested, she thought. You can always tell if people are interested by how long they spend in the house.

"You haven't seen the dining room," she told the couple, as they stood by the front door. "Or the kitchen. There's a yard at the back and a cellar below, too."

If they were leaving, she must have done a terrible job. Hearing the panic rising in her voice, Dad came out from the living room.

"Is there anything . . . ?"

"Perhaps you could leave us alone for a minute?" the man said.

"Of course."

The couple went into the living room and pushed the door to behind them.

"Did they like it?" Dad asked.

"I don't think so. They were really . . . I dunno, picky. And they didn't go to the top floor."

"Or the dining room," Dad said. "Or the kitchen. But you never know. Some people don't like to give anything away. Maybe . . ."

Before he could finish his sentence, the couple came out. Now they were all smiles.

"How much?" the man said.

Dad told him the price. The man nodded. "We'll take it."

"Fantastic!" Dad spluttered.

The man smiled and offered Dad his hand.

"It's a deal," Dad said, then shook the man's hand enthusiastically. The woman smiled politely. She still hadn't spoken a word.

"Can we offer you a drink?" Dad asked. "A celebration?"

The man checked his watch and shook his head.

"We'll be in touch," he said. "Soon."

And then they were gone.

Mum came out of the dining room. Max came running downstairs. Dad and Karen looked at each other, trying to decide if they could trust their ears.

"Well?" said Mum.

"Well?" asked Max.

"They said they'd buy it," Karen said, incredulously.

"The full asking price," Dad added, in disbelief.

Then the four of them were crowding the

hall, hugging each other and jumping up and down, making loud cheering noises.

"What were they like?" Max asked, when they'd finished celebrating.

"A bit odd," Karen whispered. "*She* never said a word."

"Nonsense," Dad said. "She's a bit shy, that's all. They seemed like a perfectly nice couple to me and they're buying our house. We can move!"

They all hugged again. Karen decided this wasn't the time to admit she didn't know the couple's name. They'd said they'd be in touch, after all.

It was only in the next few days that the Connors began to realize how tense things had been over the last six months, while they waited for a buyer. They phoned the people whose house they were buying, as well as the estate agent and their solicitor. At last they could relax. All they had to do now was wait for the buyers to return.

They waited. What did "soon" mean? How long was a piece of string? Mum and Dad quizzed Karen for any clues which might help them locate the buyers. Did they say where they were from? What did they do?

"I can't help," Karen protested, beginning to wish she'd never set eyes on them. "You were there when they came. You saw what they were like. I don't know anything."

A week became two. The estate agents confirmed that nobody had contacted them about the property, and advised the Connors to forget the buyers and keep their house on the market.

"There are some strange people out there," the woman told them. "People with no intention of buying, who visit homes for fun. They're psychos, if you ask me. Now and then they make fake offers, just to wind people up. There ought to be a law against it."

Weeks passed. Karen tried to forget about the move and concentrate on revision for her exams, but it was difficult. She could tell that, at the back of their minds, Mum and Dad both thought the buyers would be back. Karen didn't. She spent as much time as she could at Mike's. When she went there, she avoided looking down one particular street — the one they were supposed to be moving to.

Once when she was at his place, Mike showed her an article in *Hello* magazine about Bob Bosco. The comedian was pictured with his wife and beautiful daughter in their luxuriant garden, looking blissfully happy in the way that only TV celebrities could. The smug-looking daughter, Stella, was Karen's age. In the background you could see one of his guard dogs. It's not fair, Karen thought. Some people have everything. Why can't we have something?

She got home to discover that things had gone from bad to worse. The family whose house the Connors were trying to buy had just phoned. They'd had another offer. They'd need another two thousand pounds and, if the Connors couldn't complete their purchase soon, they'd sell to the new people, anyway. Dad had agreed to the new price immediately, and given the sellers some vague waffle about minor delays. But it didn't sound as if he'd convinced them. Karen could see their dream house receding quickly into the distance, already almost out of sight.

The next night was Parents' Evening at Max's school. Karen was on her own in the house, trying to revise. The exams were only weeks away. The evening was the best time to work, as most people brought their dogs in. Hearing a familiar knock on the door, she assumed it was her boyfriend. She'd told him not to come round because she had work to do, but Mike knew they'd have the house to themselves, and it must be hard for him to resist. She walked down the stairs, pleased at the prospect of his company. Until recently, being in the house on her own hadn't bothered her. But then, a lot of things hadn't bothered her until recently.

There was a second, louder rap on the door. Karen replied with an impatient shout.

"OK, you horny toad! I'm coming!" She undid the chain on the door without looking to see who it was.

"Didn't I tell you I was busy tonight, Michael?"

Then she saw them. They were dressed in an identical fashion to the way they were a fortnight before, even though it wasn't raining.

"I'm afraid my parents are out," she said, instantly regretting it.

"Doesn't matter," the man said. "Can we come in?"

"Yes. Why, yes, of course."

Karen held the door wide open, reminding herself that these people held the key to her future. She wished Mike had come round, though. She really didn't want to be alone in the house with these two, even though she couldn't put her finger on why. Nevertheless, she took the couple into the dining room.

Smiling, the man got a plastic bag out of his pocket and emptied it onto the dining room table. Wads of crumpled ten-pound notes poured out.

"This is a ten per cent deposit," he explained. "While you count it, we'd like to look at the house again."

"Yes," said Karen, nonplussed. "Of course."

They got up and shuffled up the stairs. Karen had never seen so much money before. The pile didn't take long to count. It was exactly right. She felt elated. Just at the point where she was ready to give up, everything had changed.

Quietly, not wishing to disturb them, Karen padded up the stairs after the buyers. She could hear them moving about, lifting things, talking in her bedroom.

"Here," the speaker was saying. "This will

do. And here." There was a noise in reply, but she couldn't make out the words. She was still standing outside the room when the man walked out.

"Is it all there?" he asked.

"Yes," she told him. "It's all there."

"Let's go downstairs, then." He followed Karen down.

"I'm afraid my parents won't be back for at least an hour," Karen explained. "I expect there's a lot you have to sort out with them."

The man shook his head slowly.

"Our building society will be in touch about the survey," he said. "Do you know the name of your parents' solicitors?"

Karen told him. The man got out a sheet of headed paper.

"This firm represents us," he said.

"I just remembered," Karen told him. "We don't know your names."

"Todd," the man said. "Mr. and Mrs. Todd."

His wife gave a half-smile. Dad was right, Karen thought. She's just shy. This is really happening. I can't believe it!

She pushed the front door shut behind the couple and put the chain on. She couldn't wait for Mum, Dad and Max to come home so that she could tell them, but it was too early. She wanted to ring Mike and tell him, but she didn't. She looked at the pile of money on the table and it made her uneasy. Outside, the wind roared around the house and she thought she heard the gate rattle. She went into the hall, hoping that the buyers hadn't returned — hadn't changed their minds.

Suddenly, the front door creaked open. Karen hadn't heard a key turn. It couldn't be her parents. It was too early. As she stared, a hand reached out from the dark. She froze in terror. The hand began rattling the chain. Karen screamed as loud as she could. She was too terrified to move. As the hand fumbled with the lock, there was a loud, familiar laugh. The chain sprang loose and a head appeared in the doorway.

"If you don't want me to frighten you, you should always close the door properly!"

She ran forward into Mike's arms.

Eventually Mike succeeded in convincing Karen that her worries about the buyers were groundless.

"There are lots of people who insist on paying cash for everything. They won't use banks. They keep it all under their mattress or in a wardrobe. Doesn't mean they're bank robbers, or the demon house-buyers from hell or whatever it is you've made them into in your imagination."

Karen smiled.

"You'd better go," she told him. "Otherwise Mum and Dad will think we've been up to no good all evening."

"There's still time for that, isn't there?"

Before Karen could reply, they heard the front door opening. She gave a small shudder, but it was only her parents and Max. As he walked in, Dad gave Mike a suspicious look.

"What are you doing here? Karen's meant to be working."

Dad didn't like Mike — he thought he was a bit of a layabout. Mike had been unemployed since leaving school the previous summer.

"Karen needed somebody to act as security guard, what with all the cash you keep in your house."

Karen emptied out the plastic bag onto the table once more.

"Our buyers," she said, jubilantly. "They came back!"

*   *   *

From then on, it was all frantic preparation.
This time, the estate agents told them, the
offer had been confirmed. The family whose
house they were buying were relieved the
Connors' house had finally sold. The surveyor
came round and Karen let him in. Study leave
had begun. She was at home all the time now,
revising for exams when dog noise and Mike's
frequent visits didn't get in the way.

The surveyor was a small, odd-looking man
with curly hair and glasses. His shoulders
slumped, presumably because he spent so
much time twisting and leaning over to look at
things. Karen had thought their buyers were
creepy, but being alone in the house with this
guy gave her the shivers. Eventually, after
examining every room minutely, he got a step
ladder out of his car, put on overalls, and
climbed into the loft. He stayed up there for
half an hour.

He was packing away when Dad got home.
Karen was relieved. She didn't want to have
to ask him any questions.

"Everything all right?" Dad asked, ner-
vously.

"Very nice house," the surveyor said, politely. "Very good condition. Except for the roof. You know you've had birds nesting up there?"

Karen liked to watch the birds flying to and fro in Spring.

"Well, er . . ."

"They don't seem to have caused much damage. But your slates are shot."

"How do you mean? They don't leak."

"They will, eventually. It'll be needing a new roof, I'm afraid. Sorry. Goodbye."

When he'd gone, Dad sat with his head in his hands.

"A new roof! That'll cost at least three thousand pounds. The buyers'll want to reduce the price and we can't afford to go down, not now we've had to agree the extra two thousand for the one we're buying."

The waiting began again. They were all at their wits' end. There was a statistic Mum was fond of quoting which said that buying and selling a house was the most stressful thing you could do, after death and divorce. Karen figured that at least death and divorce were over more quickly.

They waited for a phone call from the

Todds, reducing the offered price. It never
came.

"I told you," Mum said. "They're nice people. They made an offer and they're sticking
to it."

Karen said nothing. She went round to
Mike's and poured her heart out.

"You'll still love me, won't you, if I don't
come and live near you?"

"Of course I will," Mike replied, cuddling
her.

But she could tell that he was fed up with
her talking about moving all the time. It
seemed it was all any of them could talk about.
And she was beginning to believe they would
never move. Her exams had come and gone
and now she had a long wait to find out if her
results were good enough for her to go on to
the sixth form. She doubted whether they
would be. She doubted everything.

Yet when she got home, the buyers had
been round again.

"Just him this time," Mum said, sounding
jubilant. "And you know something? The reason his wife doesn't talk? She's a mute. He
told us. And there was you all suspicious!"

"He didn't say a word about dropping the price," Dad said.

Karen felt a huge surge of relief. Then she suddenly remembered that she had heard Mrs. Todd saying something the last time they came round. How could she do that if she was mute? But perhaps mute people could communicate by making noises, even if they couldn't speak. Maybe that was what she'd heard.

"So it's all going ahead?" Karen asked.

"Yes, but . . ."

There was a small problem, Mr. Todd had told them. The purchase needed to be completed within four weeks.

"Why so fast?" Karen said. "Isn't that strange?"

"He's starting a new job," Mum said. "Just down the road. That's why they chose this house, you see. He likes to be near his wife. And you know there's nothing to rent around here."

The people whose house the Connors were buying said that there was no way they could complete their own purchase within four weeks. Two months was more realistic. Reluctantly, the Connors agreed that they would move into rented accommodation for a few weeks, putting most of their belongings into storage. It seemed like a small price to pay.

The weeks before they were due to move, Dad drove the four of them to look at a faceless flat in a council estate on the edge of town. This was where they would live until their house sale came through.

"It's a 'hard-to-let'," Dad explained. "Won't cost us much. It'll do, won't it?"

They all agreed that it would. Karen found herself realizing that she didn't hate her old house half as much as she thought she did. True, there were more dogs around than there used to be, and you got the occasional drunk making a row after the pubs closed, but it felt safe, unlike the flat they were going to rent.

Moving day itself felt like an anti-climax. After all, they were moving to a grotty flat, not their dream home. It was a grey day. The storage people arrived at nine. By half past eleven, there was nothing left in the house apart from the few things they were taking to the council estate.

"Well, this is it, then," Mum said, looking

around the pine-fitted kitchen which had been her pride and joy. "Goodbye to all that."

There was a knock on the door.

"If that's the buyers," Mum said, "they're early. We're not supposed to be gone till twelve."

But it wasn't. The two men who stood at the door wore raincoats, but the resemblance ended there. One held out a police warrant card.

"Mr. and Mrs. Connor?"

"Yes," Mum said. "Is something wrong?"

"You could say that."

Karen's first thought was that the house sale had fallen apart — that the buyers were con artists, their money counterfeit. At least we've found out in time, she thought. We can stay here.

"You deposited a large sum of money in your account at the Middlemarch Building Society four weeks ago?"

"Yes," Dad said. "That's right."

"Which of you deposited the money?"

"We both did," Mum replied. "What's all this about?"

"You may not be aware," the Detective Inspector said, in a cool voice, "that any cash deposits above a certain level are notified to the police. A small portion of the money which you deposited was daubed with infra-red security markings. It was part of the ransom paid in the Moretti kidnapping last year."

Karen stared at them in disbelief. She remembered the Moretti kidnapping: the daughter of a rich Italian industrialist who was on holiday in the city had been held for three weeks. The ransom was only paid after the kidnappers cut off one of her fingers. Her captors were never found.

Mum said, "You can't think that we . . . ?"

The second detective held up a search warrant.

"I'll take a little look around."

The other nodded, then spoke in an official tone.

"We'd like you to come down to the station to assist us with our enquiries."

The first detective came back downstairs.

"The place is empty. Looks like we only just got here in time. They're doing a flit."

"This is ridiculous!" Dad said. "We're moving house. The money came from our buyers . . ."

"I'm sure there's a perfectly simple explanation," the detective said. "We'll sort it out down at the station, if you don't mind."

"Where are you moving to?" the other one asked Karen.

"The Rigsby Estate," Karen said. "But it's only temporary."

The detective gave her a funny look. Karen flinched. The situation couldn't be more incriminating. First, there was the marked money. Their solicitor had told them that a cash deposit in advance was an unusual way of doing things. Secondly, the Connors were moving to an estate with the highest crime rate in the area, parts of which were "no-go" areas for the police.

"Let's go, then," the first detective called.

Dad looked in shock. Mum was becoming tearful.

"What about our children? You can't . . ."

The Detective Inspector turned to Karen.

"Are you over sixteen, miss?"

"Yes, but . . ."

"There you are then," he told Mum and Dad. "This young lady can look after the boy. Maybe she can arrange bail for the two of you, too, if that becomes necessary. I should warn you, though, that we've frozen your building society account."

The Detective Inspector gave Karen a sympathetic smile as her parents were ushered into the police car.

"If they're in the clear we'll have them back with you soon," he said.

"What about the buyers?" Karen protested. "They'll be turning up soon."

"I doubt that," the officer told her.

"But they're the ones you want, not Mum and Dad! I always thought there was something creepy about them."

"Then it's a pity you didn't act on your suspicions," the Detective Inspector told her as his colleague waved impatiently at him.

"Please!" Karen pleaded.

"We'll send a patrol car round later," she was told. "If your buyers do exist, we'll pick them up — don't worry."

"Thanks," Karen told him as he got into the car.

"Call the solicitor!" Dad called to her. "She'll know what to do."

Karen and Max watched as their parents were driven away.

"It's a nightmare!" Max said, on the verge

of tears. "This whole thing's turned into a nightmare. Why did we have to move? None of this would have happened if we'd just stayed here — "

"Shut up!" Karen snapped. "You're not helping."

Still in shock, she picked up the phone and automatically rang Mike's number. When he answered, she poured out what had happened.

"Don't worry," Mike said. "It's obviously a simple mistake. So a few of the notes from the Moretti ransom found their way to the Todds. So what? That doesn't make the Todds guilty. It certainly doesn't make your mum and dad into criminals. You'd better ring the solicitor though, just to be on the safe side."

"Please come over."

"Of course I will."

Karen got the solicitor's number from Directory Enquiries. Her hands were shaking. When she got through, the solicitor was in a meeting, but Karen's tearful protestations finally got her to the phone. Speaking jerkily, Karen explained the situation.

"I understand," said the solicitor. "Unfortunately, I specialize in conveyancing, not criminal work. Also, I may be a witness in this

case as it seems to involve some kind of mortgage fraud. The police have been in touch with
me. It appears that your buyers' mortgage
application was fraudulent: false names and
references were used. I did warn your parents
that the Todds were cutting some corners. It
may not be the marked money the police are
interested in. They may suspect that your parents are involved in the mortgage fraud."

Karen started shouting down the phone.

"You're supposed to be on our side. You're
meant to be loyal!"

The solicitor replied calmly.

"Of course I'll arrange the best possible rep-
resentation for your parents. Let me just get
a few details from . . ."

There was a clicking noise.

"Hello?" Karen said. "Are you there?"

The line was dead. Karen dialled the number
again. Nothing happened.

"It's twelve," Max said. "That's when they
cut the phone off." Karen collapsed onto the
hall carpet and began to cry.

"Don't worry," Max said. "The police'll soon
work out that Mum and Dad are innocent.
They'll come back here and arrest the buyers.
We'll get our house back."

Karen wasn't convinced. Max peered out of the window.

"There's some more people in macs getting out of a van."

"Quick! Out the back."

They ran into the kitchen. The back door was locked. Mum had left all the keys on the dining room table. Karen went and got them.

"It's no good," Max said. "They're bringing something round the back alley."

"Let's get out through the front then."

But as they got into the hall, they saw shadows at the front gate.

"Upstairs!"

They hurried upwards, the heavy stair carpet masking the sound of their feet. Together, they crouched down on the landing.

"They're bound to come up," Max said.

"Maybe," Karen whispered. "But they never showed any interest in your room. We can hide up there. Let's see what they do first."

There was a banging on the back door. Karen heard a man's voice complain that he couldn't find a key for the door. Of course he couldn't. She had the back door key and all the

spare keys in her pocket. There was the sound
of glass breaking.

"We'll have to board it up now."

"Doesn't matter. No-one can see the back.
Come on. Get her upstairs."

Karen risked a glance downstairs. Two men
in macs were carrying what appeared to be a
carpet into the hall. The woman stood by the
door.

"Come on!" Karen hissed.

As the two men struggled to carry the carpet up the stairs, Karen and her brother made
their way up to Max's attic bedroom.

"I reckon they've got a body in that carpet,"
Max said. "They're going to leave it here."

"Don't be silly!" Karen told him. "Who'd buy
a house just to hide a body?"

There was a knock on the door. Karen listened carefully.

"Ah, sorry to disturb you," said a familiar
voice in the hall. "Is Karen Connor here? I'm
her boyfriend."

Mike must have walked in through the open
door.

"She's moved," Mr. Todd's voice replied.
"And we're busy. So get out, please."

"You see, she called me," Mike went on,

sounding nervous, "only a few minutes ago. Hey, what have you got in there?"

"I said *get out*!"

There was a sudden thudding, presumably the sound of the door being shut. Down the street, dogs began to bark. They heard nothing else.

Time passed. Although it was August, the room seemed cold. Downstairs, it had gone quiet.

"What are we going to do?" Max whispered.

"We have to wait." Karen was trying to sound calm.

"If Mike's worked out that something's wrong, he'll get help. And the police might turn up at any minute."

"You really think so?"

"They've probably let Mum and Dad go by now. They'll come for us as soon as they get out."

"But they haven't got a solicitor," Max hissed. "The police are probably still busy asking questions about the Moretti kidnapping."

"Well, what do *you* think we should do?" Karen asked.

"I think we should get away from here."

"Suppose they catch us leaving?"

Max shrugged. "I dunno. We'll say that we got left behind. Or that we've just come back to show them where we left the keys. Why should they care if we're in here?"

Karen wasn't sure. She kept thinking about Maria Moretti, chained up in a dark room for three weeks until a million pounds was paid.

"But we know they're criminals. They had that marked money."

"So what?" Max replied. "It could have come from anywhere."

Karen shook her head. "I think they must have been involved. I don't think we should risk it. Two of us . . . if they hear . . ."

"I'll tell you what," Max suggested. "I'll sneak out, go to the solicitor's, then go to the police. I'll tell them that the buyers are here and get the police to come and interview them."

Reluctantly, Karen agreed. They couldn't stay hidden in Max's tiny room forever. Maybe she should be the one to go, but she was scared.

"Be as quick as you can," she said, giving him the key.

* * *

After that it was silent. Be patient, Karen told herself. Soon the police will come, if they're not on their way already. There was more loud barking from the dogs on the street. She curled up in a corner of the empty room, which used to be so cramped. There was nowhere to hide if the buyers came looking for her. Hurry up, Max! she thought. Hurry up, Mike!

Heavy rain began to pour down onto the house. She waited, as water fell through the holes in the roof and began to drop from the attic ceiling. Downstairs, there was a lot of banging. They must be boarding up the broken back door. But it didn't sound as if they were actually moving anything into the house. The rain kept up, but the noise from the dogs subsided. Their owners were letting them in from the rain outside. It must be evening. Where were the police?

Karen thought about her parents and the luxurious house they were meant to be moving into next month. Why hadn't they been content to stay here? Why had they let these people buy their house? And what did the buyers *really* want the house for? Every guess she

made at the answer to the last question made
her feel worse inside.

The rain stopped. Every time Karen heard
a car slowing down on the street, she held her
breath. Eventually, one stopped. There was
a knock on the door. No reply. Then another
knock, louder this time. It must be the police,
Karen thought. Or it could even be one of her
parents. They'd left their keys behind, after
all. *Come on!* she shouted silently. *Knock the
door down!* But all she heard was the sound
of a car driving away.

Whoever it was must have assumed that the
house was empty, Karen decided. If she'd
thought more quickly, she could have flashed
the attic light on and off, signalling to the outside world. But what if someone below noticed? Outside, another car slowed down. The
hell with it! She flicked the switch on and off
rapidly. Nothing happened. The electricity
must have been turned off.

Karen wished she was wearing a watch, but
she had packed it, rather than risk scratching
the face while they were moving. The rain
started again and she could hear nothing else.
Once, she thought she heard another knock
on the door, but it was probably her imagi-

nation. Suddenly, there was a flash of lightning from outside, momentarily flooding the room. Seconds later, a crack of thunder followed. Dogs began to bark. From downstairs, Karen heard the unmistakable sound of a scream: a scream of terror and agony. It stopped as suddenly as it had started. Could it have been Max, or Mike? She couldn't bear it if . . . but no. It had sounded like a girl.

Slowly, it became dark. Karen shivered in the room, remembering the scream, waiting for the police to come. But they didn't. She would have to escape, but how? She had given Max the back door key, so she would have to leave through the front. They would be bound to hear her go that way. Suppose she couldn't run fast enough?

Hours passed and still nothing happened. Why hadn't Max got help? Karen wished she'd urged him to go straight to Mike's. Max was so young. If something happened to him she'd never . . . she heard the familiar sound of people walking up the street from the pub. Half eleven. Now was the time to make her move. Soon it would be quiet again and anything she did would be noticed. The door opened without a sound. Shaking with fear,

Karen crept down the stairs, trying not to let the keys in her pocket make any noise.

The house was silent. The only noises came from outside. Soon the drinkers would be gone too. Karen's body was stiff from sitting on the floor so long, but now she had to hurry. Presumably the buyers had gone to bed — if they had brought beds. Or maybe — it *was* possible — they had left. Please let them have left!

She opened the door to the landing. It made no sound. Tip-toeing along the corridor, she paused at the top of the landing, listening carefully. It was then that she heard a moaning noise. It was coming from close by — from her old bedroom.

Karen tried the door. It was locked. She remembered how the woman — the one the man said was mute — had tested this lock so carefully. Now she knew why. Forgetting her own danger for a moment, Karen felt in her pocket, carefully sorting through the keys until she found the spare one for her bedroom. Then, as quietly as she could, she opened the door.

The room was pitch black. Karen opened the curtains and looked around. A figure was huddled in the corner of the room, tied to the radiator. It was twisting around on the bare floorboards, making the moaning noises Karen had heard earlier.

"Sssh!" Karen whispered. "I've come to help you."

She leant over the shape: a girl, she could see now, tall and thin. Awkwardly, because it was so dark, Karen began to undo her bonds.

It took time. The girl continued to moan while Karen tried to separate her from the radiator. Finally, she succeeded, but at a cost. The pipe which connected the radiator to the plumbing under the floorboards came away in her hands and water began to flood out. Karen tried to stand the girl up. She didn't have time to finish untying her before someone heard. The girl made even louder noises.

"Can't you shut up!" Karen hissed. "I'm trying to help . . ." Then she realized what the girl was asking, and pulled the gag out of her mouth.

"Look out!" the girl shouted. "Behind you!"

Karen swung round as a familiar silhouette entered the room. It was the man who called himself Mr. Todd, holding a torch.

"What's going on?" he asked. "How did you . . . ?"

Before he could finish the sentence, Karen hit him as hard as she could with the central heating pipe. Blood poured from his head and he fell to the floor. She snatched up the torch. Quickly, she freed the girl's legs. As she did so, she couldn't help noticing the girl's hands, which were tied in front of her. The left one had a big bandage around the middle, where there was a missing finger.

"Come on!" Karen told her.

The two girls hurried down the stairs, towards the front door. Karen heard a stirring from the room above. She reached the door and undid the deadbolt. Then she unfastened the chain. Only then did she see the extra bar, with a padlock holding it in place. The buyers must have added it that afternoon. They were trapped.

What could they do? Start screaming? Hope a neighbour would come before one of the kidnappers did? Karen had a desperate idea.

"Follow me!"

By now she had recognized the frightened girl.

"You're Stella Bosco," she whispered, as

they hurried into the kitchen. "The comedian's daughter. I saw you in a magazine."

"Yes. Who are you? Did they kidnap you too?"

"No. I live here. Or I used to. How did they get you?"

"I'd just got out of the taxi which brings me back from my voice lessons. They grabbed me as I was walking up to the gates."

Now Karen understood why the kidnappers had bought the Connors' house. It was so close to the Boscos' that they could deposit the girl there before anyone was after them. And no-one would think of looking somewhere so near her home . . . But surely by now the police must have realized that Mum and Dad were telling the truth, even if Max hadn't arrived yet. The kidnappers would have warned Bob Bosco not to report the kidnapping, but he probably would have done so anyway. So it was only a matter of time before . . .

"Listen . . ."

Karen looked at the back door. As she'd feared, it had been boarded up. Extra locks had been added. They couldn't get out through it.

"We're going down to the cellar," she told

Stella. "At the back there's a hole, which they used to deliver coal through. We're both quite thin. We should be able to get through it. First I'll stand on your back and get out, then I'll reach in and drag you through."

Stella looked uncertain. "Are you sure it'll work?"

"It's our only chance. My brother and I used to climb through it when we were kids."

Karen opened the cellar door. She heard footsteps from upstairs.

"Hurry!"

They clambered down the steps.

"Where's the hole?" Stella asked.

Karen pointed with the torch. Then she clutched at the wall in shock. There, lying on the floor, were the bodies of her brother and her boyfriend. Their eyes were lifeless, their clothes drenched in blood. She gave a low moan.

"Come on!" said Stella, urgently. "We haven't got time to be sorry for them, whoever they are. Let's get out of here."

Speechless, Karen continued to stare at the terrible sight in front of her.

"Come on," Stella repeated. "What is it? Did you know them?"

The footsteps were getting nearer. Stella stood beneath the coal hole, one of her feet pushing Mike's bloodsoaked body aside.

"You've seen what they'll do to us," she said. "*Come on!*" She bent over, so that Karen could climb onto her back. Karen wanted to tell her to go first, that her life wasn't worth living any more. But when she opened her mouth to speak, no words came out. She put her foot on Stella's back.

The coal hole was narrower than she had remembered. She might get out, but it would be a tight squeeze. She poked her head out into the wet night. The street was silent. She pushed herself into the hole until it hurt. Her shoulders had got wider over the years.

"Hurry up!" Stella called. "They're coming."

Karen wriggled some more. In the distance, she could hear a police siren. But it meant nothing. There were always police sirens late at night. She tried not to think of her brother and boyfriend. She was nearly out. One more push. One more. The siren got nearer.

"Gotcha!"

She was yanked back into the cellar. Two men stood in front of her. The one who had

called himself Mr. Todd was holding Stella
Bosco's limp body. She had been knocked out.
The other one shone a torch into Karen's face.

"The girl who used to live here," Todd said.

"Let me go!" Karen told them. "The police
are coming."

Both men laughed.

"Finish her now," said a voice from behind
them. Karen recognized the woman who was
supposed to be mute, who was meant to be
Mrs. Todd. She spoke in a strong Italian accent.

As the police cars pulled up outside, the man
with the torch plunged a knife deep into Kar-
en's heart, then pulled it out. She was barely
alive as he threw her on top of the bodies of
her brother and boyfriend. Then, cursing his
bad luck, he and the other man dragged the
unconscious Stella upstairs. The last sound
that Karen heard before she died was that of
police sirens, as the panda cars pulled up outside her house.

Upstairs, the kidnappers undid the safety
clips on their guns. The whole operation had
been a mess. They'd be lucky to get any kind
of a ransom now. At least the police couldn't
know about the people they'd killed, or there

was no chance that they'd let them get out of here alive. If only the gang had been able to find a house near the comedian's for rent, none of this would have happened.

The kidnappers heard the police beginning to surround the house. They dragged Stella Bosco's limp body into the hall, then waited patiently, preparing to negotiate their way to safety.

Down the street, a dog began to bark.

CLOSENESS

Chris Westwood

CAMERON HAD NEVER BEEN WITH A GIRL BE-
fore, and it was beginning to show. While the
girl in the coffee shop shifted on her stool,
next to his at the bar, he gnawed the rim of
his cup. Now and then he managed a quick
sideways glance at her, but she seemed not
to notice him. That was par for the course,
though: he'd spent enough miserable nights
alone in this place to know the score. When
she finally turned purposefully and looked at
him, Cameron looked away.

He ought to be getting back soon; back to
the dingy student flat with its shabby uphol-
stery and noxious two-ring gas burner. There
were two mocks on Friday, another two early
next week, and he ought to be studying, not
wasting his evenings this way. He called for
another espresso and winced at the hot, warm-
ing sensation low in his stomach.

The girl was leaving, slipping through his fingers like so many others before her. Tall and slim, with short straight dark hair and loud red lips, she seemed impossibly unapproachable. He wanted to shout out after her, but instead it was all he could do to watch her slide from her stool, sweep up her coat and walk to the door.

He sipped at his espresso, nerves jumping, and glanced around the coffee bar. Cheap mauve-tinted lights burned over tables in shadowy alcoves where couples held hands and whispered. A dead jukebox stood in one corner with an out-of-order sign slung over it like a loud medallion. Was this as good as it got? Jesus, if only he had the wherewithal to rub shoulders with the crowds in Harveys or Raffles Tavern or any of the "in" clubs in town! Staring blankly into his cup, Cameron wondered what could have happened to the get up and go in his life. He supposed it must have got up and gone.

Then he noticed the newspaper, abandoned on the stool where the girl had been sitting. He hadn't had time to pick up the *Evening Post* tonight. Leaning to his right, clutching the bar for support, he seized it. The newspaper was

folded open at the Small Ads, among which
was a lengthy, print-smudged Personal Column. All human life was here. Two-line place-
ments from palmists and crystal-ball gazers,
birthday messages, obscure in-jokes between
friends with assumed names — Cameron read
them all with a mixture of amusement and
disbelief.

*Respectable businessman, 48, interested in the-
atre and music, seeks lasting relationship with
same.*

*Alleycat, 22, seeks Tom. Must be non-smoker,
vegetarian, into animal liberation and general
good karma. Pref. Libra but Taurus acceptable.*

At the head of the next column was a boxed
advertisement which he read twice over while
mouthing the words:

*Lonely? Bored? In need of that
special someone?
We at Forever would like to hear from you.
For years we have been bringing people
together,*

young and old alike, priding ourselves in the lasting nature of their friendships.
We are NOT like other date-link organizations! No payment unless completely satisfied! No obligations! Phone for our free brochure and videotape NOW!

Cameron scanned the ad once more, lingering over that no-obligations line for a moment, then folded the paper into his overcoat pocket. He wasn't so foolish as to fall for this — it was the kind of come-on you found in every free press newspaper. No, he would quickly forget all about it, had done so a thousand times before, was lonely but by no means desperate. The only reason he was taking the paper was that he'd missed the evening TV news. That was all.

The newspaper was still open at the Small Ads when Cameron arrived at the flat on Litton Street. As he peeled off his coat and shied it onto the bed, it spilled from his pocket, unfolding itself before his very eyes as if shouting: *No obligation! No obligation!*

No . . . obligation. He fell asleep with the words on his lips and, rising thirty minutes late

for his first college class, padded two flights
downstairs to the communal pay phone in the
hall, picked up the receiver and dialled. What
the hell! It couldn't hurt, could it? He'd read
about scores of computer dates that had
worked perfectly, and found that encouraging.
Of course they never told you the bad news,
of the thousands of mismatched flops — why
would they? — but there was no point dwelling on the down-side. Sometimes you had to
think positive. Besides, the phone was purring
at the other end.

"Forever." It was a young woman's voice,
warm and efficient. "Can I help you?"

Cameron explained through a series of stut-
ters and pauses. Smells of Indian food and stale
beeswax hung in the hall about him.

"That's fine," the girl said at last. "I'm sure
we can accommodate you. We aim to please."

"So what happens now? Do I write to you?"

"Oh, no. Just give me your address and we'll
have your special no-obligation package in the
mail this afternoon. It comes with an application form. Just fill it in and return it if you're
still interested."

"Thank you."

"No, thank *you*. It *can* be a cold, lonely world

out there and we're doing our bit to make it less so, that's all. Just remember: we're always at your disposal."

"Thank you."

"No, thank *you*, really."

He dictated his address and hung up.

Two days later, the package arrived. It came in brown wrapping paper, bearing a local postmark, and Cameron had almost completely unwrapped it by the time he'd trooped from the mail-stand in the hall upstairs to his room. Inside he found a VHS cassette, a photocopied application form, reams of promotional literature, and a full-colour Forever brochure crammed with colour stills of happy, smiling people in exotic locations, lounging beside bright turquoise swimming pools or dining in candlelit restaurants.

He turned to the video first. Seated on one end of the lumpy bed — there was no space in this dump for a sofa — he watched while a smug, spotless man in an easy chair peeled off his mirror sunglasses, flashed his teeth, then told Cameron gloatingly:

"I used to be just like you, my friend. Bored and lonely and alone. Girls would fight among themselves just to avoid me. Seven-stone weaklings would kick sand in my face."

A title appeared on the screen now, red letters vibrating against a yellow background:
ANONYMITY
And now five letters dropped out to form the word: AMITY

"You see," Cameron's host went on, "those days are long gone. Like you, I'd had enough of the old life, all those lonely nights and despairing mornings. Even work was beginning to grind me down. I was a shop-floor worker in a factory full of deafening lathes and jigsaws, and look at me now! I'm dealing with people in a way I never thought possible, with a confidence that comes from not being afraid. Because I'm *not* afraid any more, and nor should you be . . ."

It went on like this for several more minutes, until Cameron found himself watching a parade of actors and actresses — or perhaps even real people, much like those in the brochure — talking, laughing, drinking, dancing. His toes were beginning to curl. He felt envious, yet somehow strangely excited. These rôle models weren't so far out of reach after all. They were just like him, or had been once.

The sequence was scored with a soft, lulling Muzak of the sort played in hotel lobbies and airports. He thought again of the tall, dark-haired girl in the coffee shop, and how at last she'd slid from her stool and departed alone. Perhaps she'd been waiting for him?

Oh, please.

That sinking feeling again.

"And remember," the smug, spotless host said as the camera cut back to him again, "you could be on the verge of making a decision that'll change your life. Forever."

Now a cut to the title, yellow on blue:

FOREVER

And in voiceover: "No more sitting brooding in dark rooms alone. No more writing to pen-pals fearing to God they might actually want to meet you. No more tables for one! Forever at your disposal, that's us, my friend."

As the man replaced his mirror shades, Cameron reached for the remote-control handset. It took him almost five minutes to complete the application form.

Later, on Cross Street, his fingers hesitated just for a moment at the pillar box's gaping black mouth. This is really too good to be true, he thought. Surely . . . but no, sometimes you had to grasp the nettle, you had to *act*. Then the envelope was gone and there could be no turning back. Late afternoon sunlight tingling his face and hands, Cameron strode to the park, feeling strangely, delicately alive. Seated on a bench by the lake, he closed his eyes for a time, just drifting. The girl in the coffee shop passed through his mind like a ghost. He had never been with a girl before. How should he begin? What would he say?

At five he headed back to the flat, college forgotten, revision forgotten. This was important, damn it! Sometimes you had to prioritise things. But there was still one nagging doubt. It *did* all seem too good to be true. There had been nothing, for instance, in Forever's literature to explain how the agency worked, how they intended to help. It was only to be hoped they didn't employ some kind of self-help therapy in their efforts to unite people. The idea of twenty nervous neurotics gathered together in a room, suffering loneliness and claustrophobia, seemed appalling. One in a room was bad enough.

The weekend came, and so did a letter from Forever thanking him for his application, which had now been accepted. Membership, the let-

ter went on, would change his life radically for
the better. Then came the bad news. Life
membership would set him back £200. So the
cost was the snag. Already living in student
overdraft hell, Cameron wrote out a cheque
on the spot.

It was only after he'd mailed it that another
doubt surfaced and a cog began to turn slowly
way back in his mind. What did *life* membership
have to do with it? Did Forever really mean
forever?

He was halfway through the front door on
Monday afternoon, still frazzled from the first
of his mocks, which he sensed he had narrowly
flunked, when the phone in the hall started
ringing. As he snared the receiver a familiar
voice needled into his ear, and something inside his chest lurched sharply.

"Mr. Cameron James?"

"Right. Speaking."

"Forever, sir."

"Forever at my disposal, yes?"

"Ha, ha! Very good, sir." The girl's good
humour sounded genuine.

"What can I do for you?" Cameron asked.

"Actually, it's more a question of what *we*
can do for *you*, isn't it, sir? We've received

your cheque and I'm calling to invite you to
our offices. Is today convenient? I'm afraid this
is very short notice, but we're rather over-
subscribed at the moment."

"Ah." Cameron considered for a moment.
"You want me to come to you?"

"Yes, but we'll pick you up. We're keen to
explain how everything works here. We believe our clients should be prepared for an
atmosphere of — well, closeness. This will
help break the ice, that's all."

"Well, thank you. I — "

"No, thank *you*," the voice insisted. "Forever at your disposal, remember? Our driver
will be with you inside an hour, if that suits."

It did. Cameron hung up, feeling revived and
awake and somehow afraid. It was just nervous nausea. He'd gone through it a thousand
times before, while making eye-contact with
girls in the college refectory or on the bus into
town, or being faced with shop assistants who
might, just *might*, be reading his thoughts
while they served him. Good God! he scolded
himself in the shower. If that's how you feel
about a mere preliminary, how will you feel on
the first date? Shape up!

He shaved, dressed, pored over yesterday

evening's newspaper without absorbing a word. He was blindly scanning the Small Ads again when the buzzer above the door in his flat made him start.

Cameron went to the window, which overlooked the main street. Parked down below, directly in front of the building, was a sleek black stretch limo. No, it couldn't be. He blinked, but the vehicle refused to vanish. First they call you sir, then they give the full VIP treatment. Surely, if this was for real, Forever was unique. There could be no other agency quite like this.

It took only a matter of seconds for Cameron to grab his coat, close up the flat and pelt downstairs, breathless by the time he reached the front door. A uniformed chauffeur stood there, his cap held close to his chest, the smile of a doorstep salesman dawning slowly over his face. He led Cameron straight to the limo and opened the rear door.

"Forever welcomes you," he said, replacing his cap.

"I never really expected — "

"All part of the service, sir."

Soon they were cruising through town, Cameron lolling regally in the back. He

watched the town's workers moving like a tide
down the high street towards bus stops, rail-
way stations, shops. He closed his eyes but
the dream persisted. Alone no more, he
thought calmly. Closeness forever. He felt like
a prince.

"So how does this work?" he wanted to
know.

"Beg pardon, Mr. James?"

"The agency. What exactly does it do for
us?"

"With respect," the chauffeur began, hook-
ing the limo left towards Mount Temple,
"you're about to find that out for yourself. It
isn't really my place, you see, to explain. All
I can say is that none of our clients ever feel
lonely again. Dr. Ludgate will tell you the
rest."

"Dr. Ludgate?"

"The head of the Institute."

Cameron nodded, sat back. Perhaps it
would be better to wait, not to pry. Everything
in its own time. After all, Forever *did* talk of
absolute discretion; perhaps that was why the
driver was so unforthcoming. In any case, they
had almost arrived, by the look of it. He was
beginning to recognize the grand Georgian

houses in the Mount Temple district. The streets were broader here, their pavements lined with red-yellow sycamores. Even the air seemed clearer.

They pulled into the gravel drive of a large brown mansion set well back from the road. Great white stone pillars flanked the steps leading up to the front door. There were no nameplates on the wall outside on the house itself, but Cameron had passed this way many times. He recognized the building but had never known what it stood for until now. The limo came to a standstill and he was about to shoulder open his door when the chauffeur, killing the ignition and alighting from the car in a single sweep, got there first.

"All part of the service," he said, cap in hand.

"Forever at my disposal," Cameron muttered as he climbed out.

"Pardon, sir?"

"Nothing."

By the time he reached the building's main door the chauffeur was ahead of him again, the door was wide open already, and Cameron was being swept into a white, high-ceilinged entrance hall where chrome fittings glittered and shag-pile carpets whispered underfoot. Ceilings were high as clouds. There was the faintest whir of air conditioning and, softer still, a distant, insistent rumble, like a low, confused mumble of voices.

Straight ahead was the stairwell, carpeted white. Cameron started towards it instinctively. Somewhere behind him the chauffeur said quietly, "Reception first floor, Mr. James." When Cameron looked behind him again he realized he was alone.

This is it, he thought. The start of something new. A step towards closeness, away from loneliness. He took the stairs two at a time, following the carpet at the top to an open-plan reception where the secretary — blonde, gorgeous and wearing a wedding ring, damn it! — directed him to a seat and spoke inaudibly into her desk-top intercom. A few minutes later the intercom buzzed; Cameron glanced up to meet her stare.

"You can go through now, sir. Dr. Ludgate is ready."

"Thank you."

"No, thank *you*."

In the next room, Dr. Ludgate rose from the depths of his leather chair to shake Cameron's hand. Another man was seated far across the office on a leather chaise-longue. Suddenly Cameron felt infinitely small. This place seemed to swallow him up. A Persian carpet covered both the floor and the mirrored ceiling. The walls were hung with fine Impressionist paintings which, Cameron guessed, were probably originals, not cheap prints. The chair into which Dr. Ludgate guided him seemed, by comparison, almost too small, and when Dr. Ludgate slunk back into his seat behind the desk again, Cameron felt ten centimetres shorter.

"Glad you could join us," Dr. Ludgate said brightly. "There's always room for one more at Forever. By the way, Mr. James, this is my associate, David Gill."

Gill puffed a smile towards Cameron. It vapourized quickly.

"I suspect you're wondering what this is all about," Ludgate said. "The limo, the red carpet treatment . . ."

"To be honest — "

"To be *perfectly* honest, it's people like you who keep people like us in business. And for that, you deserve the very best. Am I right?" Ludgate flashed a quick look towards Gill. Gill nodded. "Believe me, Mr. James, there are many, many more where you came from. Hundreds and thousands of sad sacks who *haven't* taken the brave step you've just taken. But they will. Sooner or later they'll have to admit to themselves they could use a little help. Which is precisely why we're here."

"You've been very successful so far," Cameron said, looking about him.

"No kidding. I've lost count of the number of clients who've passed through our hands . . ." He paused and looked Cameron straight in the eyes. ". . . *en route* to a better life."

Cameron gave an appreciative whistle. "Tell me more. Like for instance, where are the *girls*?"

Dr. Ludgate laughed dryly. "Keen. I like to see you're so keen. But first come with us and we'll show you how everything works around here."

The other man, Gill, had already stood and now led the way to a full-length mirror which only became a door when he pushed it open and passed through. Ludgate laid a hand squarely on Cameron's shoulder as they followed.

"We aren't like all the rest, you know," he was saying. "We don't send our people on blind dates and we don't believe in computer dating. People are living things, for Godsakes, *not* statistics. At Forever, we believe they belong together, and it's our rôle in life to bring them together — our *only* rôle."

They were moving along a narrow, softly-lit corridor towards a plain, unmarked white door at the end. Cameron thought he could hear that same clutter of voices again, closer yet still indistinct.

"So where does it all begin?" he asked. "How does this actually work?"

Ludgate's large pinkish face formed a smile. "I can see you're a one for the questions — curiosity is a very good sign, a healthy sign if it means a genuine interest in others. You could be one of our prize clients one day, Mr. James. Actually, *we* make the introductions, right here on the premises. It seems to us more discreet this way."

"Really? You just bring people here and throw them together?"

"In a manner of speaking, yes. Of course we supervise to begin with, but generally we

like to see these things take their own course.
Are you game?"

Cameron swallowed dryly. "Well, I've come
this far."

"That's the spirit."

They were standing at the door now, Gill
watchful and silent, poised over the handle.
"Whatever your tastes," Dr. Ludgate went on,
"I'm sure you'll find someone that suits you
here. You'd be amazed how many of our clients
have become — well, committed to spending
the rest of their lives together. Don't you think
that's quite an achievement?"

Cameron did. He thought also that Dr. Ludgate's easy manner and the opulent world that
was Forever would help him enormously. If
only he'd stumbled across this years ago. He
was definitely moving on now, leaving doubt
and fear and frustration behind at long last.
Perhaps for the first time he was beginning to
relish the challenge too, to relish the idea of
breaking — being broken — from his shell.
There were no more cogs of uncertainty rattling round in his mind now; no qualms at all
until the moment Dr. Ludgate gave the nod
and Gill flung open the large white door.

After that, they were inside a white room

that to Cameron seemed more like a laboratory than an office. In fact it *was* a laboratory.
Computer consoles winked endless streams of
data; programmers carrying clipboards bustled
about collecting printouts. Cameron could
even detect the faintest after-scent of disin-
fectant, he thought, and something sweetly,
very mildly sour beneath it, like spoiled meat.
The sounds were there too — louder, more
clearly like voices than ever. But the sight that
caused him to freeze in his tracks was straight
ahead, at the far side of the room. It was
enough to send a thousand cogs into motion
inside his head, and none of them made any
sense.

He saw a huge reinforced door marked:
DISPOSAL ROOM 1.

He saw a girl on duty in front of it, dark and
demure and pretty in her white doctor's coat;
a girl whose easy, effortless smile made him
instantly cold. It was the girl from the coffee
shop, the girl whose evening paper had
brought him here in the first place.

Speechless, Cameron looked at Ludgate,
whose own smile had faded. So had the doctor's touch on Cameron's shoulder. His touch
had become something else altogether now.

Gill's hands trapped Cameron's arms, tying tight knots of pain at the back of his neck.

"As you see," Ludgate said as they neared the Disposal Room door, "we also believe our clients need a degree of encouragement — prompting, let's say — at least to begin with. After all, this is quite a huge step to take, from hermit to life and soul of the party. Some might develop cold feet. But just think of the benefits. You'll never feel lonely again as long as you live. You'll always have company."

"Forever at your disposal," the girl added flatly, wiggling a thin silver key in the lock. In a moment she had flung the door wide.

Cameron cried out, but at once the sound was swallowed by the noise just in front of him. Those muffled voices were no longer muffled; they weren't, as he'd imagined, lowered in conversation but raised in an agony of cries and screams — a hundred voices, two hundred, perhaps twice that number. He could be more certain now because he was inside the room. And soon he would be one of them too.

The last voice he heard from outside was Ludgate's. The words were unclear. He turned and saw the trace of a smile crease the man's lips, and then the door was swinging shut, thundering shut. After that he was alone with the mob.

At first all he saw was a riot of thrashing white arms and legs and dark eyes that pierced him with wild, hungry stares. The clients were packed in here so tightly they were crushed wall-to-wall. Some were unable even to stand. Others, their clothing shredded to rags, were skinny, emaciated, with strange jutting pot bellies. Then there were those with madness more firmly fixed in their eyes. But they all screamed as one, and Cameron dropped his gaze hurriedly, unable to look.

As he did so, he saw a strip of white bone somewhere under the pounding feet, and something which might have been a splash of red meat. Then he saw the girl, crouched low against the wall on his side, near the door. Dark blonde hair fell in straggles across her face, and she brushed it aside to look at him. Her eyes, green and tearful, seemed filled with a longing he recognized almost at once. He knew that feeling too: she'd been trapped on the outside too long. It was something he had in common with her. Already he knew her as well as himself.

Very gradually she smiled through her tears, and cute little dimples puckered up in her cheeks.

He thought that perhaps he would talk to her — just sit right down and start in with a chat. She looked like she needed a friendly voice right now, and despite the screams of those who were trapped here forever, Cameron suddenly had all the courage he needed.

THE RING

Margaret Bingley

THE MOMENT KATE SET EYES ON THE RING she knew that she had to have it. She wasn't normally interested in old-fashioned jewellery, but this was different. It was a small gold band with a ruby-red stone set in the centre, surrounded by tiny diamond-like chips, and its timeless elegance appealed to the Kate she longed to be. That Kate was tall and slender, not short and slightly plump; she was witty and popular at discos and parties, instead of quiet and always on the fringe of things. This ring seemed to symbolize everything she hoped she would one day become, and she had the ridiculous feeling that if she could own it — actually wear it on her finger — then all of these things would be possible.

The jewellery shop itself was new. It had opened only a month ago, and although Kate and her friends passed it every day on their

way home from school they'd never really
studied the window display before. Kate had
left school early that day for a dental appointment and was dawdling along killing time, so
she'd stopped to look in the window, and once
she had looked she was lost.

Her sixteenth birthday was in two weeks'
time, and so far she hadn't been able to decide
what she wanted as a present from her mother
and Steve. Steve was her stepfather and Kate
liked him, but she was still close to her dad.
He'd remarried too, straight after the divorce
six years earlier, and he and his second wife,
Lizzie, lived a few streets away with their four-
year-old twin sons, Jake and Ben. They'd give
her money for her birthday — they always
did. Kate's mum, Louise, said it was because
they were too busy with the twins to find time
to choose a present, but she and Steve always
gave Kate presents and so possession of the
ring was a real possibility.

Before she mentioned it at home she took
her two best friends, Samantha and Clare, to
look at the ring. They didn't seem as im-
pressed as she was.

"It's a bit old-fashioned," said Samantha.
"They've got better rings on the jewellery stall

in the market on Saturdays. Really shiny ones, and much bigger than that."

Kate, normally a very placid girl, felt an unaccustomed rush of anger. "I don't want cheap tat. I want a nice ring!" she snapped.

Samantha and Clare glanced at each other in surprise and Clare decided not to say she thought it was hideous, and more like something her grandmother would wear. "It's certainly different, Kate," she said tactfully, "but I bet it's dreadfully expensive. Antique jewellery always is."

Kate hadn't thought of that and her stomach did a kind of dip, as though she was on a rollercoaster ride at the fair. "How expensive?" she asked.

Clare shrugged. "I don't know; probably a couple of hundred pounds. Isn't there a price tag on it?" The three girls peered into the window, but nothing on display was priced.

"That's sure to mean it costs a fortune," said Samantha. "It's like that posh dress shop on the High Street. They don't show prices either, but Mum says they charge you just for walking inside!" Both she and Clare laughed. Kate didn't. To her friends' astonishment she was opening the shop door and marching inside, leaving them alone on the pavement.

"She's in a funny mood," said Samantha.

Clare sighed. "Probably because she hasn't got a boyfriend." Then they smiled at each other, confident that they looked good and that boys were attracted to them. "She'd be okay if she'd dress better and chat more," continued Clare, "but she doesn't seem to try."

"She's fed up because Jeff hasn't asked her out yet," muttered Samantha. "If only she'd come out of her shell a bit she'd do much better. There's nothing really wrong with her."

"No, but then there's nothing really right either!" exclaimed Clare, and Kate's two supposed friends collapsed in giggles on the pavement outside the shop.

Inside the shop, totally unaware of her friends' derision, Kate was standing in front of the glass-topped counter, her heart thumping erratically as she faced the most handsome man she'd ever seen. She'd expected the owner to be a small, wizened old man with glasses, not a tall, dark man in his early thirties whose brown eyes skimmed over her with seeming admiration while his lips parted in a warm smile.

"How can I help you, young lady?" he asked gently. His voice was deep and rich, like an actor's.

Kate swallowed hard. Her friends were right, she thought; everything inside the shop spoke of money. She must have been stupid to imagine that her mum and Steve could afford to buy anything that was on sale here, and if she hadn't been transfixed by the magnetism of the owner's gaze she would have turned and run.

"It's the ring!" she blurted out.

His eyes widened a fraction; the dark pupils seemed to expand as he stared at her with even more interest, so that a small tingle ran through her. "Which ring would that be?" he asked softly. "I do have quite a few."

Kate knew this was true, yet she had the totally illogical feeling that he knew which ring she meant, and knew that it was meant for her just as certainly as she knew it. "The old one with the red stone in the middle. It's in the left-hand corner of the window," she said in a rush.

He nodded. "Ah yes, *that* ring. It is very

attractive, and has quite a history too. Many, many people have worn that ring."

"How do you know?" asked Kate.

He gave a short laugh. "Because it's old, of course!"

"I suppose that means it's very expensive," said Kate despondently.

"Well now, that depends on what you call expensive. In terms of money, I would say it was quite cheap."

Kate frowned. She didn't understand how it could be expensive in any other way apart from money. Expensive meant things cost a lot. As far as she knew there wasn't any other way in which the ring could be expensive, but then Kate was not yet sixteen and she still had a lot to learn.

"How much is it?" she asked bravely, bracing herself for disappointment.

"I take it it's for you?" queried the owner.

"Oh yes! You see, it's my sixteenth birthday soon, and this would be the most perfect present, only we don't have . . . Well, my parents are divorced and that. I mean, we aren't poor or anything, but I've got stepsisters at home now, and twin half-brothers at my dad's and so the money has to stretch further and . . ."

She stopped, appalled at what she'd said. How could she start telling a perfect stranger all these things about her family, things she never discussed with anyone, not even Samantha and Clare?

The man nodded. "It happens a lot these days. I tell you what, you try it on for size and if it fits, if there's no need for any alteration, then you can tell your mother it's . . ." He stopped and stared at her for a moment. "How about twenty pounds?" he suggested.

Kate shivered with a mixture of excitement and fear. Twenty pounds was exactly what Steve had told her they could afford to spend. She'd felt a bit put out because Laura, his twelve-year-old daughter from his first marriage, had got a computer for her birthday and that had certainly cost more than twenty pounds, but then she'd pushed the thought away because Steve always treated her like his own daughter in other ways.

"Twenty pounds would be perfect," she said to the man.

He turned towards the window and brought the ring up to the counter. Close to it looked even better. Although Kate knew it couldn't be real gold for that price, the band had a warm glow about it, and the red stone in the middle was dark while the small pieces of glass round it glittered with reflected light.

"Which finger did you want to wear it on?" he asked her.

Without thinking, Kate held out the ring finger of her right hand. He took the ring from its box and slid it carefully over the nail. Kate held her breath in painful excitement. It looked far too small to fit her finger, and she wished she'd said the little finger, where it might have stood more of a chance. She felt her hand begin to tremble in the man's, and his unusually long fingers tightened, holding her hand steady as the ring continued its progress. It seemed to the startled Kate that the ring actually changed shape as he moved it, expanding to fit her and gliding smoothly over the knuckle until it came to rest just beneath the joint.

She stared down at it, and her whole hand felt warm. Somehow the ring seemed to change the look of her hand in the way she'd hoped. It seemed slimmer and more elegant, less the slightly pudgy hand of an adolescent and more that of a rich lady of leisure.

"A perfect fit!"

Kate could hear the satisfaction in the man's voice, and she smiled at him. "It's gorgeous. I think it looks even better on than off. Will you keep it for me until Mum can come in and pay for it?" she added anxiously.

"Of course. The ring is most definitely yours."

"I'd better take it off," said Kate, but it fitted more snugly than she'd expected and proved difficult to move.

"Allow me," said the shop owner, and once again his long fingers closed round her hand and another tingle ran through her as he slid it off easily and put it back into its box.

"You'd better have my name," said Kate breathlessly. He nodded, writing down her details as she gave them to him, but she had the weird feeling that he already knew everything there was to know about her.

As he placed the ring back in its box, now labelled with her name, she had one small moment of unease, a premonition that perhaps this had all gone too easily. Somehow the price seemed too low and the fit too perfect, but she brushed the thought away. How could anything be too good?

"I'll tell my mum tonight," she promised the

man. "She should be able to get here tomorrow, or Saturday at the latest."

He nodded, obviously quite confident that
the ring would be collected and paid for. At
the doorway, Kate stopped for a moment.
"Why is it so cheap?" she asked hesitantly. "I
mean, even coloured glass costs money, and
it's so well made. Everything looks real."

The man nodded. "Lots of things that seem
real aren't; people too, I find. Besides, I never
said it was a cheap ring!" He laughed softly,
more to himself than to Kate.

"It is really old though, isn't it?" persisted
Kate, wondering why on earth she was doing
this when she wanted it so much. It was just
that there was definitely something making
her uneasy.

He looked steadily at her. "Very old," he
confirmed. "Perhaps you'd be happier if I
charged you more?" he added.

"No!" exclaimed Kate. "No, honestly. I suppose I can't believe my luck."

"I hope you enjoy your birthday," he said
evenly, and as the door closed behind her he
smiled to himself before putting the boxed ring
carefully into his safe. He considered that he'd
just made a very good sale.

Outside the shop Samantha and Clare were far from happy. "You were ages!" complained Clare as they hurried home. "What on earth were you doing?"

"I tried it on, and it fitted," said Kate happily.

"How much?" asked Samantha sourly.

"Only twenty pounds, so that's all right. It means I can have it!"

Her friends had never seen her so elated. Neither of them would have been seen dead wearing the ring, but they didn't say as much to Kate. It would only cause trouble and at least she'd get a decent present this year. Last year she'd got a hairdryer, which they'd all agreed was pretty mean, even if it did free the other one for the rest of the family. Hairdryers were boring, everyday necessities. Rings, even weird ones, were proper presents.

As Kate had anticipated, her mother and Steve were delighted to hear that she'd found a present she wanted, and the very next day her mother went off and collected the ring. When she got home, Louise told Steve that it was very pretty, but not at all what she'd have expected Kate to choose.

"I'm sure it's valuable too," she added when he'd buried himself in the sporting pages of the newspaper. "For one thing it's hallmarked, and the stone in the middle looks remarkably like a real ruby."

"Perhaps the guy doesn't know what he's doing," said Steve, without much interest. "The main thing is we got it for twenty pounds and Kate will be happy."

"I suppose so. It's only . . ." Louise's voice trailed away when she realized Steve still wasn't listening. She couldn't blame him. Why look a gift horse in the mouth? And they were lucky that Kate was such an easy-going girl, never resenting the fact that Steve's two daughters had more spent on them, or that her father's second wife didn't ever seem that pleased to have her to stay for more than a day at a time.

Sometimes Louise felt really sorry for Kate, but at other times her daughter's lack of self-confidence irritated her. Steve's girls were so different. They were both lively and quick, did well at school and were popular. They were easy to be proud of, but they weren't her children and Kate was her own flesh and blood. She knew that the divorce hadn't helped, but sometimes she found herself wishing that Kate was less like her father, both physically and mentally. Not that she'd ever let her daughter know how she felt. It was one of those secret things that she kept firmly locked away most of the time, and she knew that Kate had absolutely no idea that she disappointed her mother.

On the morning of her birthday, Kate was awake early and for the first time in several years she felt fizzy with excitement. Today she'd actually get the ring, and as it was a Saturday she could wear it all weekend. She was hoping to wear it at school as well, but if they had a routine clampdown on jewellery she'd have to leave it off for a while. It never crossed her mind that this might not be possible.

At eight o'clock all the family piled into her bedroom, her mother carrying a tray with cups of tea and biscuits, the usual birthday-morning routine.

"Happy birthday, darling!" she said with a wide smile.

"Happy birthday, Kate!" shouted Sara, Steve's ten-year-old daughter, while Laura kissed her on the cheek and said: "You're getting really old now, Katie!" which made them all laugh.

Lots of presents and cards were put on her bed, but Kate simply couldn't wait any longer and fell on the tiny, beautifully wrapped parcel that her mother had put beside her. She tore desperately at the glossy paper and ripped off the gold bow, like a starving person falling on food.

"Steady on!" said Steve, made slightly nervous by the feverish way his stepdaughter was scrabbling at the present, but when she lifted the lid of the box he saw the ring and whistled softly to himself. No wonder Louise had been surprised at the price. It did look really valuable, a genuine antique.

Even Sara and Laura were silenced by the ring's beauty, and watched breathlessly as Kate slipped it over her finger. For Kate this was one of the best moments of her life. She couldn't remember when she'd last wanted something so much and she stretched out her hand, noticing once again how much slimmer it looked with the ring in place.

"It's beautiful, darling!" said her mother. Kate lifted her head for a kiss, and as her

mother's smiling face moved towards her she
quite clearly heard her say: *What a pity her
fingers are so fat.*

Kate gasped. Her mother's lips hadn't
moved, she was still smiling and moving towards her, and yet the words had been said.
Kate drew back, tears prickling in her eyes.

"Darling, whatever's wrong? It looks lovely,
doesn't it, Steve?"

"Fantastic!" agreed Steve heartily. "Come
on, Kate, give me a birthday kiss." Bewildered, Kate turned towards Steve. He had his
arms outstretched and he too was smiling, but
even as he smiled she heard him say, *And
unless I'm very much mistaken, I'm the only
man apart from her father who'll kiss her today.
She really ought to do something to smarten
herself up.*

Kate's throat seemed to be closing and
there was a hammering at her temples. She
gave a tiny cry and drew back from both Steve
and her mother. They glanced at each other
in consternation, but Sara and Laura, totally
unaware that anything was wrong, pushed
their present into Kate's hands.

"Here you are, Katie. We hope you like it,"
said Sara.

With hands that were shaking, but from shock now instead of excitement, Kate undid their present. It was a tube of liquid foundation, one of a new range she'd been thinking about trying. Her mother was always saying that young girls didn't need much makeup, but Kate knew that the girls who did best at parties were the ones who were heavily made up. You couldn't be sophisticated with the freshly scrubbed look of a ten-year-old.

"Do you like it?" asked Laura, jumping up and down.

"It's great. Thanks."

Sara began to examine the ring on Kate's hand. *We thought it might help cover your zits!* she sniggered.

Kate drew back her hand sharply. "I don't get zits!" she protested.

They all looked at her in surprise. "No one said you did, Kate," said her mother gently.

"Sara did!"

Sara looked frightened and backed away from Kate's bed. "I didn't! I didn't say anything!"

"Mum?" Kate's voice was high with fright.

Sara continued to stare at her stepsister in astonishment, and even as Kate's mother reassured her that no one had mentioned zits, Sara's voice rang through Kate's head as clear as a bell.

She heard what I was thinking!

Kate's head whipped round and she looked at Sara in amazement. Suddenly her head was full of voices. Her mother's sounded irritated as she muttered: *What on earth's the matter with her now? Why can't she be happy for once?* while Steve's was lighter although his words were desperately hurtful: *Thank God she's not my own daughter!* In the background she could hear both her stepsisters wishing she'd hurry up and go to her father's for the rest of the day, and in a sudden moment of blinding clarity, Kate realized what was happening.

It was the ring.

She tried to remember what the man in the shop had said. Something about nothing in life being what it seemed, not even people. Kate was beginning to understand what he'd meant by that.

She was about to tear the ring off her finger when the voices subsided. Everyone was still looking at her oddly, and there was a strained atmosphere in the bedroom, but thankfully the voices had stopped.

"Are you all right, Kate?" asked her mother anxiously.

Kate nodded. There wasn't anything she could say to them to explain her behaviour, and perhaps it wasn't the ring. Maybe she'd got over-excited about the present and imagined it all, or at the very worst picked up some of their thoughts by accident, like a mistuned radio or something. It couldn't really be the ring; that was ridiculous. In fact, now that everything was normal again she decided that nothing had happened. She'd imagined it all. She must have done, otherwise how could she continue living in a house where the people who were meant to love her best said one thing and thought another?

Kate shook her head. "I'm sorry; I don't know what happened. I felt really odd but I'm fine now. Must have been too much excitement."

"Do you still want to go to your dad's?" asked Louise. "Would you rather spend the day with us?"

Inside Kate's head she heard someone groan. "No, honestly, I'm fine," she said quickly. "Besides, Lizzie's cooking a special lunch. I can't let them down."

"She wants to get her hands on her birthday money!" joked Steve, breaking the tension in the room. Everyone laughed. After that, Kate opened the remaining presents, looked through her cards, and when the others had gone pulled on her dressing gown and went into the bathroom to shower.

It was then that she discovered the ring wouldn't come off.

It had gone on easily enough, but now it was gripping her finger like a vice, and the harder she tugged the tighter it seemed to get. She put some soap round the edge and tried to ease it over the joint, but that didn't work. In the end, with Sara hammering on the door saying she wanted to use the loo, she had to give up and shower with it on. She was terrified it would get spoilt but when she stepped out of the shower cubicle the ring was bone dry, and once again quite comfortable on her finger.

The scene in the bedroom had affected everyone, and although they all tried to keep the birthday atmosphere going they didn't quite succeed, so it was with some relief that Kate finally left to walk to her father's for lunch.

"Have a nice time!" called her mother. "And remember you're going to that disco with Samantha and Clare tonight, so you'll need to be back by six."

"I know," replied Kate.

"Hope you get plenty of money!" laughed Steve. Kate turned back to smile at him. *It's the least they can do, considering how little they have to see of her, the lucky swine!* she heard him add, yet his mouth was closed and he was simply standing watching her go, his arm round her mother's waist.

The smile died on Kate's lips. This time she knew. There was no longer any point in trying to fool herself. She was hearing what people were thinking, and it had all started when she put the ring on. She was mortified to realize that Steve resented having her around the house so much, and angry because it was her house after all. She'd lived there with her mum and dad right up to the divorce, and if anyone should feel resentful it was her, not Steve, who'd not only moved in but brought his daughters with him. Quickly she ran through the gate and into the street.

*   *   *

All the way to her dad's house Kate kept pulling hard at the ring, but it wouldn't move, and her finger was now red and sore. It was impossible to work out how it had ever gone on that morning.

Lizzie was already waiting with the front door open when Kate got to the house. Jake and Ben were hanging on to their mother's skirt and stared at their big stepsister in their usual solemn way.

Lizzie smiled. "Happy birthday, Kate! Your father's just had to pop out for a moment. Have you had some nice presents?"

Kate nodded, disappointed that her dad wasn't there to kiss her and give her one of his warm, reassuring hugs, but she stretched out her hand and showed Lizzie the ring. "I got this," she said quietly, surprised to see that the ring looked quite loose and that her skin was no longer red round it.

Lizzie's eyes opened wide. "That's beautiful!" she exclaimed. As she bent down to pick up Jake, who'd started to grizzle, Kate heard her add, *God knows how they could afford that! Louise is always bleating on that Brian doesn't pay enough maintenance for Kate, but that must have set them back a couple of hundred.*

Kate's lips tightened, and although she knew that she wasn't supposed to have heard, she couldn't help saying casually; "I saw it in an antique shop the other week and it only cost twenty pounds."

"Really? That's amazing! It looks so real," said Lizzie's mouth, while Kate heard her add, *What a little liar she is. I suppose Louise told her to say that.*

Kate wanted to scream at Lizzie. She felt like telling her to stop saying one thing and thinking another because she could hear every thought that went through her head. Then she realized that it could be quite useful to be able to read people's thoughts. She'd always suspected that Lizzie didn't like her. Today she'd probably find out, and then she could confront her father with what she had learnt. He was always saying Lizzie liked her a lot and he'd probably be shocked to find that he was wrong.

At that moment his car drew up and he hurried towards her. "Happy sixteenth birthday, Kate! You're quite the young woman now. Don't you think she looks older, Lizzie?"

Lizzie laughed as they all went inside. "She's got a beautiful ring from Louise and Steve," she said, her voice a little too bright. Kate showed the ring to her father. He leant over her hand and examined it closely.

"That's quite a present! Make sure you don't lose it," he said slowly.

Kate felt like saying that she could hardly lose it when it wouldn't come off, and anyway she wasn't a careless person, but before she could utter a word she was stunned to hear him thinking, *Next time Louise comes on the phone nagging for more money I'll tell her to pawn the damn ring. What a stupid extravagance for a sixteenth birthday! No doubt Steve paid to show me up. Perhaps I should have got her more than thirty pounds from the bank just now. It's lucky the cashpoint was working.*

There was real resentment in his thoughts, and Kate took a step away from her beloved father. Had he forgotten her birthday until this morning? Did he begrudge paying anything for her? And didn't any of them consider her feelings? She was beginning to think that she was nothing more than an expensive nuisance whom no one really wanted. Kate had never felt so alone.

At that moment Ben pushed himself forward and held out a card. "Happy birthday," he mumbled, while Jake hid behind him. Kate bit her lip to stop herself from crying, opened the card and took out three ten-pound notes. She swallowed hard. "Thanks, Dad. That's really generous. Thanks, Lizzie."

"We've got a tree house now — come and see," said Ben. Kate went willingly because she didn't think she could look her father in the eye right at that moment. The tree house was a sturdy, well-crafted one set in the large oak at the bottom of the garden. "Only our friends are allowed in," said Jake.

"Am I your friend?" asked Kate, and then wished the question unasked, but the two small boys nodded and she heard one of them saying: *I love Katie.* She nearly wept with relief and hugged them close, realizing gratefully that they were still too young to lie like the adults.

Lizzie had cooked Kate's favorite lunch: melon, followed by pork chips in cider and apples, with a sticky chocolate pudding to finish. Kate was now so terrified of what she might hear that she was afraid to make any kind of conversation, and if it hadn't been for the twins it would have been a very silent meal.

She gets more boring by the month, she heard her father think as he lifted his glass of wine to toast her birthday. *I shall have to mention it to Louise. She doesn't seem to have any idea of how to chat or have fun.* He smiled at his daughter over the rim of his glass. "Happy Birthday, sweet sixteen!"

Somehow Kate managed to smile back, but inside she was crying out with the pain of her father's betrayal. She'd always felt so secure in his love.

"Why don't you take Kate out for a walk this afternoon, Brian?" suggested Lizzie as she stacked the dishwasher. "The twins need a rest, and it would be nice for the pair of you to have some time alone together."

Kate watched her father carefully. His mouth smiled, but his eyes didn't as he nodded. "Sounds like a good idea. What about going along by the river? We could take the dog."

"Fine," agreed Kate apathetically, waiting for what was to come.

At least the dog will enjoy itself, she heard her father think as he took the lead off the peg in the hall. *The exercise will do Kate good too. She looks out of condition. I'll get Lizzie to tell her about that new aerobics class later.*

This was too much for Kate. "I'm not fat!"

she shrieked, unable to bear it all any longer. "I'm perfectly fit and I don't want to go for a walk with you ever again. I'm just sorry I cost you so much, but if I do badly in my exams I'll leave school and get a job in a shop or something so that you can stop paying a penny, then Jake and Ben can have another tree house or two with all the money you save."

Lizzie stood in the middle of the hall with her mouth open in amazement. "What on earth's going on?" she asked.

"I'm leaving!" shouted Kate. "I hate you, I hate him, and I loathe aerobics!"

"Aerobics?" asked a bewildered Lizzie. Her husband was too stunned by what his daughter had said to reply, but the loud slamming of the front door told him that Kate had really gone. He couldn't understand where all the anger had come from. Kate was normally so quiet. Nor could he work out how she'd known anything about the aerobics, but assumed Lizzie must have said something without him prompting her.

He sighed. Inside he felt rather guilty. Once he'd been close to his daughter, but now the twins took up most of his time and energy. They were a lively pair, full of chatter and far easier for a man to deal with than a withdrawn teenage girl.

"What happened?" demanded Lizzie more forcefully. "Did you say something unkind to her on her birthday?"

"No!" he replied testily. "I've no idea what got into her. It must be her age. All teenagers get moods. Anyway, she'll soon be back. She's left her card and money behind."

Out in the street, Kate finally began to sob. Her tears just wouldn't stop, not even when people started to stare. She knew that she had to go somewhere but she couldn't go home. She wouldn't give them the satisfaction of knowing that the visit to her dad had been less than perfect. Distraught, she decided to go to see Clare.

Luckily Clare was in, doing her nails in her bedroom and listening to her favourite group on her CD player. "Hi! Happy birthday," she said casually, then looked at her friend more closely. "What's the matter? Didn't you get the ring?"

At that, Kate began to cry even more. The ring! She wished she'd never set eyes on it. If only she could get it off she'd throw it in the

river and never ever want anything so badly
again, but as she pulled at it she felt the ring
begin to tighten again and her sobbing became
hysterical.

Clare put her arms round Kate. "Hey, it
can't be that bad. The ring looks great on you,
and we're going out tonight. Is it your step-
mother?"

"No, it's . . ." Kate couldn't go on. She
couldn't begin to explain because all at once
she realized how stupid she'd sound. Clare
would never believe that the ring enabled her
to hear people's thoughts. Unless she showed
her, thought Kate suddenly. If she got Clare
to think of an object then told her what it was,
that would prove she was telling the truth. "It's
like this," she said between sobs. "I . . ."

God, I hope she hurries up, she suddenly
heard Clare thinking. *Jeff's due here in half an
hour, and she'll go mad if she finds out we're
going out together, especially as she's hoping to
get off with him at the disco tonight. How can
I get rid of her?*

With a cry, Kate pulled herself free of
Clare's embrace. "How *could* you?" she
shouted.

Clare frowned. "How could I what?"

"Go out with Jeff. You *are* seeing him, aren't you?"

"Is that what all this is about? No, I'm not. As though I'd do something like that behind your back! We're friends, aren't we? I know how much you fancy him, so why would I do something like that? Anyway, I'm going out with Mark at the moment."

Kate stared at her supposed friend. Clare's face shone with sincerity. She looked hurt and surprised, but not at all guilty, and the lies were flowing from her mouth so easily that Kate guessed she must lie a lot. Everyone lies, she thought to herself. The man in the shop was right. She knew that now, and knew too that she'd paid a high price for the ring, just as he'd said.

"Forget it!" Her voice was weary. "I'm going home now."

Thank heavens for that! thought Clare, while aloud she said: "Are you sure you'll be all right? I mean, you're welcome to stay for as long as you like."

"No, I've got to go."

"See you at the disco then, about eight."

"I'm not coming," said Kate flatly. "I don't feel well."

"But it's your birthday," protested Clare, at the same time thinking: *Samantha will be relieved. Now we won't have to sit around keeping her company just because it's her birthday.*

"Would you tell Samantha for me. I hope she won't be too disappointed," said Kate, and saw a faint flicker of disquiet in Clare's eyes.

"Of course; but she'll be really upset. It won't be the same without you."

"I know exactly how she'll feel," said Kate as she left Clare's room and trailed down the stairs.

When Kate got home she told her mother that she thought she had 'flu coming on and went off to her bedroom. Louise took her daughter some hot lemon and two paracetamols and said what rotten luck it was on her birthday, but finally Kate was left alone, although not in peace. She'd had no peace since the ring went on her finger.

For hours she lay in bed fiddling with it. It was no good. The ring wanted her as badly as she had once wanted it. Kate looked into a future where she would always know what people were really thinking. She knew that in the end it would drive her mad.

When Louise and Steve went to bed, Louise paid her daughter a final visit. "Daddy rung earlier," she said, smoothing Kate's hair off her hot forehead. "He was very worried about you rushing off the way you did, but I explained about the 'flu and he sent his love and said you must go round again as soon as you're better. Your money's still there."

"Right," mumbled Kate, keeping her eyes closed.

"You should have told him you felt ill," continued Louise. Kate didn't reply. Her mother's thoughts ran on: *How dare he criticise me because she's not very sociable. It doesn't come from my side of the family. His mother wouldn't step outside her own front door from one year's end to the other.*

I hate them both, thought Kate vehemently as her mother's thoughts continued.

Sometimes I wonder how I could have had such an uninteresting daughter. At her age I was always off having fun.

"Goodnight," said Kate shortly.

"Goodnight, darling; I love you," said her mother gently.

It was an unbearable lie. Kate knew that she couldn't live like this any longer. No matter how difficult it proved to be, the ring had to go.

She waited until the house was silent and then crept down the stairs in the darkness and made her way through into the kitchen where the sharp cooking knives were kept. She'd get the ring off her finger if it was the last thing she did . . .

It was her mother who found Kate lying dead and cold on the kitchen floor the next morning. No one ever worked out what she was doing down in the kitchen in the middle of the night, or how she came to sever the ring finger of her right hand nearly in two with one of the kitchen knives, but in the end it was decided that it must have had something to do with her fever.

The actual cause of death was a combination of loss of blood and shock to the nervous system, and everyone was totally devastated. As an added mystery, no one was ever able to

find the much-coveted birthday ring that had
brought her — as her mother told everyone
who'd listen — such happiness on her last day
on earth. They even tried to find a replacement
to put in the coffin with her, but the jeweller's
shop had closed down and a large "Premises
to Let" sign was attached to the window.

On the very morning of Kate's funeral, as the
stream of black cars followed the hearse to
the crematorium, a young woman, Grace,
wandered along the streets of a small town
many hundreds of kilometres away, arm in arm
with her new husband.

Grace knew how lucky she was. She'd mar-
ried a handsome man who was rich and adored
her. They stopped in front of a small, newly-
opened antique jeweller's shop, and Grace's
eye was caught by a small gold ring with a
beautiful ruby set in the middle, surrounded
by tiny diamonds. It seemed to call out to her.

"Look, isn't that beautiful!" she said softly.

Her husband glanced down at her adoring
face. He wasn't nearly as rich as Grace believed, but he had already insured his young
wife for a great deal of money and was busy

working out how to dispose of her without suspicion falling on himself.

"Would you like it, sweetheart?" he asked.

"Oh yes! Yes, I would."

"Then let's go inside. If it fits, you can have it. I'd do anything to make you happy, Grace. You know that."

Grace glowed with pleasure while her husband wondered how much the ring would cost and how soon he could put his plan into operation and collect the insurance money on his wife's death.

They walked into the shop. "Please let it fit," thought Grace to herself.

A tall, dark man in his early thirties looked up and smiled at them. "How can I help you young people?" he asked gently.

BONE MEAL

John Gordon

Eunice did not want to show herself to anyone, but when the door chimes rang and no one went to answer them she ran downstairs barefoot and opened the door. A young man stood in the porch.

"Hi," he said.

She caught her breath. He was obviously a student, someone Richard knew. Richard must have sent him.

"Hi," she said.

He was tall, and his head brushed the ferns trailing from a hanging basket in the porch. "Nice flowers," he said, and looked beyond her into the hall. "Nice place you've got here."

He was incredibly corny, but she gave him a tiny smile and was just about to ask him in when he put down the large hold-all that was slung from his shoulder and held out a plastic card for her to see. Eunice did not have good eyesight, and she had to lean forward and squint. "Has Richard sent me a postcard?"

The young man mimicked her rudely, squinting back. "Who's Richard?"

"He's my . . ." But Eunice broke off. Richard was no longer her boyfriend — or so he said. She straightened. "So who are you?" she asked.

"That's what the card's for, lady. It's me." He held it up alongside his head and leant forward so that his face was rather too close to hers. "That's me picture in the corner. See?" He squinted again, laughing at her.

"You don't have to do that. I can see quite clearly it's you."

He drew back and looked at her, calmly taking her in from the face framed in long black hair down to the bare feet. "Pity I'm not Richard," he said.

Eunice knew she should have closed the door in his face. His grin was not altogether pleasant, too predatory, unlike Richard's much gentler expression. But Richard had hurt her. She hated Richard. She lowered her eyelids modestly.

"I know identity cards don't mean much," the boy said, "but it's genuine. And I'm not pretending I'm doing this for charity."

"Doing what?" She raised her eyelids and saw that he was crouching beside the hold-all and had opened it.

"I sell things — cleaning materials, dusters, mops, oven gloves. That's how I pay me way, and it ain't charity. It's the only job I can get. Are you a student?" he asked abruptly.

She nodded.

"You'll soon know, then. It's hard to get a job."

She did know. Richard was already writing letters. She smiled suddenly at the thought of him in jeans and sweatshirt pleading on doorsteps like the boy at her feet. How she would make him suffer for the way he had spurned her.

The boy misinterpreted her smile. "Don't believe me, then," he said. "And I ain't a burglar either, no matter what people think of us." He held up a plastic package. "Look, I got a cleaning pack here — two dusters, wash leather, demister cloth — three-fifty. You can't do better than that anywhere."

Suppose this boy was Richard, what would

she do? She smiled sadly in the shadow of her hair and at the same time advanced one of her small bare feet, as if by accident, to the edge of the doorstep. "I'm afraid I don't want anything," she said.

He was gazing at her toes. Five little piggies. "You on holiday?" he asked.

"The long vac," she said.

He looked up. His mouth was thin-lipped and rather cruel, she thought, and his eyes had a smiling challenge in them. "Well, is there anything you want?" he said. "Anything at all?"

"I don't think so." She lingered over the words.

"You never know your luck." His eyes held hers until very deliberately, she lifted her foot and pointed with her toe.

"What's that?" she asked. She knew he had to obey her, and he picked up one of the plastic packages.

"Oven gloves," he said. "So you won't get burnt."

"Nothing ever burns me." Her smile was sweet, but it was a lie. Richard had hurt her. "I won't let it happen."

"Never?" He was taunting.

"Never ever." She had stirred his interest

but had not yet humiliated him. Now was the time. "You haven't anything I want," she said. "Nothing at all."

She had stepped back and was about to close the door when he stood up. "Hang on a minute, Miss."

She had expected menace in his voice and was disappointed there was no threat in him. His expression was earnest. "Have you had a lot of people like me around?" He jerked his head to indicate the rest of Jasmine Close. "Woman up the road said she was sick of the sight of us."

"You're the only one as far as I know."

"I was only asking because a mate of mine used to do this patch and I ain't seen him in a long time. He's just vanished."

"Nothing to do with me, I'm afraid." She kept all interest out of her voice as she added, "Sorry." It was an insult and he knew it. The pale skin round his eyes became pink with anger, and for a moment Eunice wondered if she was afraid of him but then, behind her, she heard footsteps in the hall and she stood to one side to let her mother take over.

Mrs. Barnes stood squarely in the doorway and looked at the boy. She was not tall but, despite the delicate colours of her flowered dress, she was as solid as a boulder, and as silent.

"Missus." The boy dipped his head respectfully.

Mrs. Barnes had a mouth that nothing would prise open if she willed it shut. She said nothing.

"Is she your daughter?" The boy had not given up, and he indicated Eunice, who stood half-sheltered by her mother's shoulder. "She wasn't sure if you wanted any of this stuff." He gestured towards the bag at his feet. "I've got some nice lines." He stopped and was beginning his sales patter when Mrs. Barnes spoke.

"You can take it away," she said.

The boy looked into the glint of her glasses and saw there was no chance for a sale. "If that's how you feel, lady." He zipped up his bag and lifted it. "I'm just trying to make a living."

"Go and make it somewhere else."

He had begun to turn away, but the sharpness of her voice prodded him into turning back. "Just one thing, lady, and it won't cost you a penny. I was asking your lovely daughter

if she'd seen a mate of mine around here, doing
what I'm doing. She said you might know him,"
he lied. "Bloke about my height, bit skinny,
long hair . . ."

"I don't answer the door to you people."

He grinned then, and again looked beyond
Mrs. Barnes to Eunice. "Lovely," he said.
"Real crumpet. I don't know where you get it
from, gorgeous."

Mrs. Barnes was quivering, but she kept
her voice under control. "I think you had better
go," she said, "or I'll fetch my husband to you."

"Dear, oh dear," he said, and sauntered
away down the drive between the bright flowerbeds as the door slammed at his back.

Eunice had always thought of the hall as her
favourite place. It was here she had played
when she was small, enjoying the coolness of
the parquet floor when running about had made
her too hot, and when her dolls had been
naughty, which was often, she would put them
one by one on the stairs so that they gazed
sorrowfully out between the banisters like a
rising tier of prisoners in solitary confinement
while she, the one good girl, curled up on the
thick rug below like a cat, content with herself.

The hall was the heart of the house, and she possessed it. Except that once in a while, if she had wrinkled a rug, or shaken petals from the flowers on the hall table, her mother, in a white rage, would drive her upstairs, slapping at her legs until her flesh was red and she was weeping. Now, as the door still shook, she gazed at her mother's set face, and the old fear returned.

Mrs. Barnes breathed deeply, mouth shut so tight her lips were invisible, and Eunice felt the coldness of the parquet against her bare feet as she waited in terror to be blamed.

"Is he gone?"

Her mother's voice made her start, and she put her face closer to the crinkled glass of the window into the porch. It was, as far as she could see, empty and the driveway beyond it lay in the sun as silent as the rest of Jasmine Close. "He's nowhere," she said, and she turned to see that her mother's grim expression had changed.

"He's very lucky, is that young man."

"Lucky?" She was startled by her mother's sudden good humour.

"He's lucky your father didn't see him."

Eunice had perfected a little gurgling laugh

she had had since childhood. Men liked it. "Daddy couldn't hurt a fly," she said, and her mother laughed with her.

There was — there had always been — a barrier between Eunice and her mother, and to find themselves laughing together suddenly brought tears to Eunice's eyes and, even more surprisingly, her mother noticed.

"Is something wrong, Eunice?" The words came out reluctantly. She and her daughter had never shared confidences.

Eunice shook her head.

"So why are you crying?"

Eunice could not bring herself to confess. She could never tell her mother, who had slapped her legs until they were red, that she longed to hug her. The thought of the resistance that there would be in her mother's solid body repelled her so sharply that she found herself saying, "It's Richard. He makes me want to cry. All the time. He's the one."

Mrs. Barnes was silent for a moment and Eunice felt that she might be about to open her arms to her daughter, but it did not happen. "Is that why you're spending so much time in your room?" she said.

"Perhaps." Eunice hung her head. "Maybe it is. I don't know."

Again a pause. Mrs. Barnes was finding it difficult to continue. Then she spoke. "Has he done anything to you?"

"No!" Eunice cried. "No! You don't think I'd let him, do you?" She glared, maybe for the first time in her life, at her mother. There was a spark in the eyes behind the glasses, and an added grimness to the mouth.

"Because I saw what you were doing to that boy just now."

"What!" Eunice was indignant. "I don't know what you mean."

"Your bare feet," said her mother. "You know very well what you were doing."

Eunice opened her mouth wide. "I don't believe this! Bare feet? Are bare feet indecent?"

"Wriggling your toes under his nose."

"My toes!" Eunice began to laugh and then her laugh became a cry and she ran weeping from the hall, through the sitting room and out through the open french windows into the garden at the back of the house. There were secret places there, arbours and winding paths, but it was to the summerhouse, half hidden beneath a tree, that she ran and curled up with her head between her knees and sobbed. It was the fault of the boy at the door. He should never have looked at her feet like that. He was hideous, lecherous, just like Richard. She hated men.

She may have fallen asleep, she wasn't sure, but very gradually she found herself listening to a rhythmic sound as if something was slicing at the ground outside. It was a peaceful, gentle sound and she listened for a full minute to her father hoeing before she dried her eyes on her T-shirt and stepped into the sun.

Mr. Barnes was not a large man. His wellingtons, she often thought, looked too big for him, but she was fond of the old woollen cardigan he wore. She remembered that when she was small she would creep up behind him and reach into the pocket for the sweets he kept there. And he wore the same old hat with the crinkled brim that he pretended he'd stolen from a scarecrow, and she had believed him. She stood on a strip of lawn between the flowerbeds and waited for him to see her.

He raised his head. "Hullo," he said, and then came the pun on her name. "You nice

girl?" He had pronounced her name like that
when she was really small, telling her that he
had made it up for her. "You nice?"

"Maybe." She was sullen, pouting.

"Have you been crying?"

"Maybe. Maybe not."

He looked at her carefully. He knew she
would speak to him when she was ready. She
always did. He carried on with his work.

"What are you doing?" she asked.

"Hoeing."

"No." She was cross. She wanted his attention. "What's that stuff you're using?" He
was sprinkling the earth with something from
a bucket and then hoeing it in. He didn't answer. "It's nasty," she said. "I don't like it."

"I'm not surprised. It's not for little girls."

"I'm not little." But she had her hands behind her back and was swinging her long hair
petulantly. "I'm a big girl."

He glanced quickly at her and went on sprinkling and hoeing. "Girls don't want to have
anything to do with dried blood and bone
meal."

"Blood?" She made a horrified face. "Ugh,
Daddy. How could you!"

"It makes the pretty flowers grow." He
looked quickly at her, but she had lost interest.
"Where are your shoes?" he asked.

"Don't you start getting on at me as well."
Her voice was a gentle wail, but he couldn't
see her face because it was shadowed by her
hair. "I couldn't help the way that boy looked
at me."

"What boy?"

She had been watching her toes curling on
the turf, but the sharpness of his voice brought
her head up. Beneath the grey stubble of his
moustache his teeth showed, and his eyes
were bright and foxy.

"Daddy!" she protested. "You frighten me."

"Has some boy been troubling you? Insult
you, did he?" He held the bucket by its brim
and shook it. She drew back in distaste.

"That smells, Daddy. Take it away." He
lowered his hand. "No, he didn't trouble me
at all." Now it was her own eyes which were
careful. Her father had hardly raised his voice,
and his only gesture had been to hold the
bucket so tightly that his hand shook, but his
nostrils were white and his lips were gummed
together in an uncomfortable shape. She had
never seen him as angry as this. Perhaps her

mother had been right; he really was a fierce protector.

"It was only a boy at the door," she said, watching for his reaction. He was wooden. "He was quite nice to me, really. It was Mummy who was suspicious of him."

His head jerked slightly to one side. He was listening.

"But he was only trying to sell me something," said Eunice.

"Uh." Her father shook his head as if ridding himself of troublesome insects. "Those young men are a pest. They're round here all the time."

"That's not what Mummy told him." Once again Eunice saw that she had his attention. "He told her he was looking for a friend of his who used to come here, but she said she hadn't seen anyone at all."

Her father shrugged, and turned to resume his hoeing. "She wanted to get rid of him, I suppose."

"But she needn't have been so cruel, Daddy." He ignored her. She picked up the bucket he had left on the grass. "He was only trying to find his friend who had vanished."

"Well, he came to the wrong place, I'm afraid." The hoe sliced earth methodically.

"I was just wondering," said Eunice, and she tipped the bucket to sprinkle its contents alongside his hoe, "if my mummy didn't get my daddy to chase a nasty boy away."

"That sort of young man doesn't take much notice of me," said her father.

"So there *was* someone?"

The hoe suddenly bit deeper. "What if there was? He insulted your mother, and I ticked him off. He became very abusive, but I think I gave him a bit of a fright. I don't want to talk about it."

Eunice laughed. "My little daddy!" She tipped the bucket up. "He's a knight in shining armour!" She kissed him on the cheek. "And so modest he doesn't even want to admit it."

"I don't want it mentioned. Not to anybody. It's embarrassing. And watch your feet — you don't want them mixed up in that stuff."

Some of the bucket's contents had fallen on her toes. It was black and sticky, and she had to rub her soiled feet on the grass before it came off.

*   *   *

Eunice never dreamt at night. It was as if her
mind, like the pure oval of her face, fitted so
perfectly into the space allotted to it that there
was no room in it for anything but herself, and
thus there was no need to dream. Her days
were her dreams, and her nights were blank.
But tonight, as she lay awake, an intruder
spoiled the smooth harmony of her feelings.
Richard.

He was as tall as the boy who had been
fascinated by her on the doorstep, even taller,
and he, too, had fallen under her spell. It was
not that he had been easy to charm — far from
it. He was rather aloof, quiet, with little to say
to girls — at least not pretty ones with kit-
tenish ways. He had ignored Eunice, and she
wanted him.

If it had been Richard who had come to the
door today she would never have advanced
her dainty toes; he would have scorned anything so crude. But she had known exactly how
to tilt her head away from him as he spoke so
that he saw the curve of her cheek below the
fringe of her dark eyelashes, and on cold days
she would hug herself to keep warm but shiver
and bury her face in her scarf to the very tip

of her small nose as she listened to him talking with his friends. He noticed her then.

She sat up in bed. It was agony to think of him. He had fallen in love with her. Wildly. He had become her servant. She said his name aloud, and moaned.

At the window she leant out. The summer night was full of mysteries. But there was no Richard. Suddenly, one day in the cafeteria, with no reason, he had deserted her. He was sitting with his coffee and all she had done as she approached him was to draw the tip of one slender finger along the table edge as he watched, and then playfully touch the tip of his nose. "Oh for God's sake!" he had said, and left her standing there.

Eunice opened her bedroom door. The house was silent and indifferent to her. A sharp prickle of pain came to the corner of her eyes, and then the balm of tears welled up and overflowed. She hated him.

Downstairs, in the kitchen, she did not switch on the light but reached into a cupboard for a glass. She touched something soft. There were no glasses. Her mother must have changed things around. She switched on the light. There were dusters in the cupboard. She was about to close the door when she realized there were a great many dusters — an orange stack of them that filled the whole depth of the shelf. And the stack was very neat. The dusters were new, unused.

"Mummy," she murmured, "what on earth has got into you?"

The rest of the shelf was even more surprising. It was filled with transparent plastic packets. She took one out. It was a cleaning kit with dishcloths and wash leathers. There were a dozen of them.

Eunice giggled. Her thrifty mother must have found a bargain she could not resist. Mrs. Barnes had few weaknesses, and this was something new. Eunice began to gloat. It was something she could use. "Oh, Mummy," she whispered, "you *will* be sorry."

She tried the other cupboards. There was a pile of new dish mops, twenty pan scourers, a column of tins of floor wax and, in a drawer, ten pairs of oven gloves. Richard had been charmed once to see her put bulky oven gloves over her small hands. He had said it was like seeing a little girl walking about in her mother's high heels. He really did love her, still, no matter what he said.

She lifted a large, brightly striped glove and put it on, examining her appearance. There was something inside the glove. She took it out and looked at it, frowning. Then, forgetting her glass of water, she went back upstairs and sat with the object in her hand. She was still looking at it when she fell asleep in her chair.

Next morning Eunice found her mother polishing the dining room table. "Is that a new polish?" she asked. "It smells lovely."

Her mother's small features were buttoned up as she concentrated on her work. "You can have a tin to take back with you," she said.

"Have you got some to spare?"

"I think so. Somewhere."

Eunice curled her legs under her as she settled in a deep armchair and clutched a cushion to her. The room was exactly as her mother wanted it: dark rosewood furniture, glass-fronted book cases and china cabinets, stately flower vases and subdued ornaments, and the french windows, framing the picture of the garden outside, were reflected in the long table where her mother toiled.

"I came down for a drink of water last night," said Eunice, "but I couldn't find a glass."

"I've changed things around," said Mrs. Barnes. "Did you get what you wanted?"

"Oh, yes." Eunice giggled and quoted the boy her mother had chased away the day before. "I got *cleaning materials* galore. Stacks and stacks of them."

Her mother ceased polishing. "There's a new place just opened," she said. "They sell things dirt cheap."

"No wonder you didn't buy anything from that boy yesterday. None of them ever stood a chance with you, did they?"

Her mother detected a hidden meaning in the words, and she remained motionless with both hands, one holding a duster, resting on the table top. She regarded her daughter, and Eunice, hugging her cushion, gazed back.

The silence between them was suddenly, but quite distantly, broken by a sound from the garden. It was a squeal like an animal in pain.

"What's that?" Eunice gasped. Her eyes and mouth were round.

"It's only your father." The interruption had brought Mrs. Barnes back to normal. She moved from the table to a book case.

"But what's he doing?" The squeal came again, but this time it was accompanied by a rattle and the buzz of a motor.

"He's putting twigs through his shredder, that's all."

Eunice understood. "Is that the thing like a chimney at the bottom of the garden?"

"Of course it is!" Her mother was brusque, on the point of losing her temper. "Don't tell me you haven't seen that before."

Eunice threw aside her cushion. "I'd love to see it working!"

"I wouldn't bother him if I were you." Her mother barred the way to the open french window. "You know he doesn't like being disturbed."

"But I want to." Eunice, gathering that her mother did not wish her to go into the garden, sulked. "I want to see what Daddy's doing."

"Stop being so childish. And for goodness' sake get some shoes on your feet."

"Very well, Mummy." Eunice fetched a pair of shoes from the hall and gave her mother a sly grin. "But I'm not the only foolish one around here."

"What do you mean by that, my girl!" Her mother's face had hardened and her gaze was stony but, for once, Eunice faced up to her.

"It's silly to buy as many dusters as my mummy does."

"I've told you . . ." Mrs. Barnes, now in a cold fury, took a step forward but Eunice continued, still smiling. "And silly to buy so many wash leathers, and pan brushes, and tins of polish, and . . ." She broke off and then, lowering her voice and with something of her mother's hardness in her face, said, "Are you going to tell me where you bought all those things, or . . ."

She waited for a reply but none came. "Because," Eunice resumed, "if you're not going to tell me, I'm going out into the garden to ask Daddy if I can borrow the car."

"You'll be wasting your time. You know very well he won't allow you to have it."

"You think so?" Eunice put a hand to the pocket of her jeans and took something out. She held it towards Mrs. Barnes, who reached for it but found it was held just beyond her reach.

"Where did you get that?"

Keeping her distance, Eunice circled her parent. "Oven gloves," she said, and stepped out into the garden.

*   *   *

The garden was large for Jasmine Close but
so hemmed in by trees that it was secluded
and secret. With its humps of flowers and
smooth lawns it lay in the sunshine as if pleased
with itself, as perfect as her mother's dining
room. But Eunice knew it as a place of cunning
walks and hidden nooks, a place that reflected
her father's patient and unexpected mind.

The buzz of the machine led her to a little
clearing among shrubs where her father had
his compost heaps and tool shed. As she came
closer she saw him feed something into the
top of the green funnel that rose to the height
of his shoulder, prodding it down with a stick
while the grinder at its base clattered as it
chewed and spat out fragments into his wheel-
barrow.

"Daddy!" she called but, knowing that he
did not like to be taken by surprise, she
stepped back behind the bushes and called
again.

The machine was switched off, and she went
forward slowly and timidly, peeping around the
bushes to see him standing beside the barrow,
turning over the chippings with a fork.

"May I come in?"

"Only if you nice girl." The small, round glasses that he wore when he was gardening made a twinkling circle around his eyes as he smiled.

She went forward. "Honestly, Daddy, it's just like coming into a lion's den. And what are you doing?"

"Mixing up my compost with these shredded twigs."

"Not blood and bone meal like yesterday? It did smell awful."

"All used up, my pet." He wheeled the barrow towards her and they went back in the direction of the house. "I'm just going to mulch these roses." He put a forkful of compost at the base of a bush. "Did you come to see me for anything special, Eunice?"

She knew he hated lending anything that belonged to him, but she gave a little cough and said, "May I borrow the car, Daddy?" He didn't look at her. "Just for today, while mine's being serviced."

"Can't you wait?" He dug the compost in.

Eunice knew this might be his response, but she desperately needed a different car. Too many people would recognize hers where she intended to go today, and she didn't want to be seen.

She watched him digging for a moment and then she said suddenly, "Is that a piece of bone?" A spiky, pale fragment had come to the surface.

"It could be." He covered it.

"And where's the blood, Daddy? Has it all soaked away?"

It was then that he straightened and looked at her. "My little girl has a very morbid imagination."

"So has my mummy." Eunice gave a sly chuckle. "She told me a lie just now."

Her father thrust his fork into the lawn and rested his arms on it. "Now then, Eunice, you know your mother doesn't tell fibs."

Solemn and innocent, Eunice went on, "But she just told me there's a place in town that sells dusters and things ever so cheaply, and I'm sure there isn't."

He stroked his moustache down over his lips as he smiled. "Now there's a thing," he said, as if humouring a child. "That's a whopper of a lie."

"But she's got stacks and stacks of things

in her cupboards and I'm sure she didn't buy them."

He asked her what sort of things.

"You know what I mean, Daddy — the things those boys sell at the door." He shrugged, but he was listening. "You know what boys I mean; one of them is missing."

"I don't see what that's got to do with us, Eunice."

She lowered her eyes and wiggled her shoulders. "Daddy," she murmured, coaxing him, "you know when you used to chase me and pretend you were a lion." He was silent, so very gradually she opened her eyes wider and gazed at him from under her eyebrows. "Well, I think you *are* a lion — a real one."

"Eunice." His voice was very soft. "What are you trying to tell me, dear?"

"Those boys are ever so cheeky," she said. "Very, very cheeky."

He breathed in deeply, pulling his shoulders back.

"Was one of them cheeky to Mummy?" His knuckles, grasping the fork, had whitened, and she realized for the first time what large hands he had for a man of his size. "And did you chase him away?"

His voice was a bark. "Absolutely not!"

She drew back, cowering. "You frighten me, Daddy."

"You talk nonsense, Eunice. Dangerous nonsense."

"I don't see what's dangerous about it — he must just have run away and left his bag behind." She smiled. "And you know what Mummy's like — she can't bear to see anything go to waste."

"Well, whatever she's got tucked away indoors, there's nothing to prove it belonged to that young swine — whoever he was."

"I think his name was McNulty."

"Hmm?" He frowned. "What makes you say that?"

She took something out of her pocket and looked at it. It was a plastic card. "It says John McNulty — and it's got his photograph."

"Give me that!" He leant over and snatched at it, but she held it out of his reach.

"Oh, you really are a lion, Daddy. Mummy and I have nothing to be afraid of when you're around, have we?" She handed him the card.

"Where did you get this?" His voice was still sharp, but he was pale.

"In an oven glove in the kitchen, Daddy. May I have the car now, please?"

With the car keys in her hand Eunice glanced back just as she turned the corner of the house on her way to the garage. Her father stood where she had left him. He was looking towards the house. Inside the open window, her mother stood in the dining room looking out. They made a perfect picture, Eunice thought: he with his lush garden, and her mother with her gleaming furniture.

It was easy. It was a thrill. It was a daydream coming true as she drove out of Jasmine Close, out of town, and found the motorway. The grey Datsun Sunny with its unmemorable number plates hummed smoothly through the forty kilometres of sunlit countryside to the city. She left it in the big, open car park at Sainsburys and strolled towards the store just to make sure.

It was a gamble, of course, but today was her day, and Eunice was confident. And Richard was there, just as she knew he would be, his long arms showing a lot of wrist beyond the cuff of his brown supermarket jacket as he lifted cans and bottles to fill the shelves. He was as studious doing this as he was in college, and she watched him for a while. He was very courteous to a woman who asked him a question, and Eunice felt a pang of jealousy when he smiled in his slow manner and the woman, obviously liking him, smiled back. Not that it mattered. He would soon be sitting in the Datsun, and Eunice would have him to herself.

He was surprised to see her as he walked across the car park on his way home.

"I was just shopping," she said.

"Were you?" He was suspicious.

"I'll give you a lift home." He didn't live far away.

"I can walk."

"Please." Her eyes filled with tears and her hand held his. He feared a scene, and angled himself into the little car.

She drove fast, and at the big roundabout took the wrong turning.

"Hey!" he said. "I go the other way."

"Oh, hell!" She bit her lip. "I forgot."

"Turn back, can't you?"

"I can't, I'm on the motorway." The slip road joined the dual carriageway and she accelerated. "It's such a pity you can't drive,

Richard. I could have let you take the wheel. It's miles to the next turn-off. I *am* sorry, Richard, I really am." She felt his eyes on her and knew the sort of slow, mistrustful stare he was giving her. "But wasn't it strange that we should meet like that?"

"Very." Now he watched the road ahead and for a full minute was silent. "That's one you missed," he said.

"One what?"

"One turn-off."

"Oh, did I? I'm so sorry, Richard."

"And you can slow down, Eunice. I'm not going to jump out. Where are we going?"

She allowed a tear to trickle down her cheek.

"You're very cruel, Richard. I just wanted to talk."

He didn't answer, and he no longer looked at her. He folded his arms and watched the road, and when they drove into Jasmine Close he got out of the car and followed her indoors without protest.

Eunice walked brightly into the kitchen. "Hullo, everyone!" Her parents sat at the table. They had, she guessed, been there for some time. Her father was still in his gardening clothes, and the table was bare, except for a plastic card that lay between them. For a moment they regarded her silently and then, with a jolt, they saw the figure of Richard loom behind her.

"You know the boy at college I told you so much about?" Eunice was beaming. "This is Richard." She saw her mother's hand swiftly cover the plastic card and draw it towards her. "Oh, don't worry about that, Mum. Nobody will ever know."

Her father got to his feet. His boots were at the back door and, standing there in his socks, he seemed even shorter than usual. "This is my daddy, Richard."

Reluctantly but politely Richard held out a hand. He was about to do the same to Mrs. Barnes, but she sat where she was and he tilted his head to her, making it almost a bow. She did not like him.

"You wouldn't believe it, Richard," said Eunice, "but my daddy's a wild animal. So you'd better be careful how you talk to me."

She laughed, but Richard managed only a thin smile. It was Eunice alone who seemed to be enjoying herself. She proceeded to make the atmosphere even more tense.

"Do you know what they've been up to while I've been away at college? You'd never guess." She waited for Richard to shake his head. She saw he was hating every minute, and this misted her eyes and made her words more frantic. "You know about the poor young men who come from door to door selling dusters, don't you? Well, one of them was nasty to my mother." Mrs. Barnes stiffened and began to object, but her daughter quietened her. "It's no use denying it — Daddy told me." She turned to Richard. "My daddy chased him off." She paused. "And that's not all."

"Eunice!" Her father came forward and slapped the table with his hand, startling everyone. "I'll have no more of this!"

"But, Daddy," she pouted, "I was only telling Richard how you look after us, Mummy and me." She lowered her voice. "And that boy was so frightened he dropped his bag and ran . . . and he's never been seen again!"

There was a deathly silence in the kitchen. Eunice watched Mrs. Barnes slowly slide the card from the table and hold it in her lap. Then she said, "So now you know what to expect, Richard. Shall I show you the garden?"

In the summerhouse she sat down and patted the bench at her side. He shook his head and remained standing. "Aren't we going to talk, Richard?"

"I don't think so." Tall, slightly stoop-shouldered, he stood with his back to the garden, his hands in the pockets of his jeans. "We don't have much to say to each other, Eunice."

She craned forward, looking up at him. Her eyes were large and damp, and her lips were inviting. "You used to say you loved me, Richard."

He was suffering. He rubbed at the floorboards with the toe of one of his worn trainers. "I'm sorry, Eunice. I just want . . . I mean I think it would be better . . . if we didn't expect so much of each other."

"What's wrong with me?" It was a wail.

"Nothing, Eunice. Nothing at all. You're very nice." He had taken a breath to say more, but she suddenly stood up and put her arms around his neck. Her lips were searching for his when she saw his distaste. And she also saw something he could not. Beyond the flowerbeds someone was crossing the lawn. She clung tighter, pleading to be kissed. He tried to free himself, but she struggled wildly and fell backwards, pulling him with her. They slid from the bench to the floor and her skirt came up. They were a tangle of legs and arms when she cried out, squealing with fear, "Get off! Leave me alone, Richard! What have you done to me! I hate you, hate you, hate you!"

She just had time to fling her arms wide before her father's spade came down across Richard's neck. Two blows were not necessary, but she stood and watched while her father made sure.

Later, having tea with her mother in the kitchen, Eunice listened to the shredder. Sometimes it was muffled as it chewed something soft, and then there would be a rattle as it disposed of something more brittle.

"Is he nearly finished?" Eunice asked.

"I expect so," said her mother, and Eunice got up and ran down the garden.

"Let me do the last bit, Daddy," she said.

He stood, holding something that dripped. She held it by its hair and lowered it into the funnel. The machine swallowed it and mumbled for a while, rolling it around, but then the blades hit on the hard bone, and the head shrieked.

"I wanted to hear him suffer," said Eunice.

THRILLERS

D.E. Atkins
- ☐ MC45246-0 Mirror, Mirror $3.25
- ☐ MC45349-1 The Ripper $3.25

A. Bates
- ☐ MC45829-9 The Dead Game $3.25
- ☐ MC43291-5 Final Exam $3.25
- ☐ MC44582-0 Mother's Helper $3.25
- ☐ MC44238-4 Party Line $3.25

Caroline B. Cooney
- ☐ MC44316-X The Cheerleader $3.25
- ☐ MC41641-3 The Fire $3.25
- ☐ MC43806-9 The Fog $3.25
- ☐ MC45681-4 Freeze Tag $3.25
- ☐ MC45402-1 The Perfume $3.25
- ☐ MC44884-6 The Return of the
              Vampire $2.95
- ☐ MC41640-5 The Snow $3.99
- ☐ MC45680-6 The Stranger $3.50
- ☐ MC45682-2 The Vampire's
              Promise $3.50

Richie Tankersley Cusick
- ☐ MC43115-3 April Fools $3.25
- ☐ MC43203-6 The Lifeguard $3.25
- ☐ MC43114-5 Teacher's Pet $3.25
- ☐ MC44235-X Trick or Treat $3.50

Carol Ellis
- ☐ MC46411-6 Camp Fear $3.25
- ☐ MC44768-8 My Secret Admirer $3.25
- ☐ MC47101-5 Silent Witness $3.25
- ☐ MC46044-7 The Stepdaughter $3.25
- ☐ MC44916-8 The Window $3.25

Lael Littke
- ☐ MC44237-6 Prom Dress $3.50

Jane McFann
- ☐ MC46690-9 Be Mine $3.25

Christopher Pike
- ☐ MC43014-9 Slumber Party $3.50
- ☐ MC44256-2 Weekend $3.50

Edited by T. Pines
- ☐ MC45256-8 Thirteen $3.99

Sinclair Smith
- ☐ MC45063-8 The Waitress $3.50

Barbara Steiner
- ☐ MC46425-6 The Phantom $3.50

Robert Westall
- ☐ MC41693-6 Ghost Abbey $3.25
- ☐ MC43761-5 The Promise $3.25
- ☐ MC45176-6 Yaxley's Cat $3.25

Available wherever you buy books, or use this order form.

THRILLERS

Nobody Scares 'Em Like
R.L. Stine